DEAD WRONG

GRAVE TALKER SERIES BOOK SIX
ANNIE ANDERSON

DEAD WRONG

Arcane Souls World

Grave Talker Book 6

International Bestselling Author

Annie Anderson

Edited by Angela Sanders

Cover Design by Tattered Quill Designs

www.annieande.com

BOOKS BY ANNIE ANDERSON

THE ARCANE SOULS WORLD

GRAVE TALKER SERIES

Dead to Me

Dead & Gone

Dead Calm

Dead Shift

Dead Ahead

Dead Wrong

Dead & Buried

SOUL READER SERIES

Night Watch

Death Watch

Grave Watch

THE WRONG WITCH SERIES

Spells & Slip-ups

THE ETHEREAL WORLD

PHOENIX RISING SERIES

(Formerly the Ashes to Ashes Series)

Flame Kissed

Death Kissed

Fate Kissed

Shade Kissed

Sight Kissed

ROGUE ETHEREAL SERIES

Woman of Blood & Bone

Daughter of Souls & Silence

Lady of Madness & Moonlight

Sister of Embers & Echoes

Priestess of Storms & Stone

Queen of Fate & Fire

I'd only known of the name Nero for less than a week and I was already tired of it. Pinching my brow, I squeezed my eyes shut and prayed for patience. I wasn't going to get any, but it was the thought that counted, right?

"Please tell me you have more than a hunch on this," I muttered, trying not to scream at the three women standing in my foyer. I hadn't had a good night's sleep since Aemon spelled me into a mini coma what seemed like months ago, and coffee was no longer cutting it.

Dahlia St. James, Harper Jones, and a decidedly altered Shiloh St. James stood in the Warden house entryway, spilling their guts about a rash of witch abductions—ones they were blaming on the nefarious, yet still unknown, Nero.

Evidently there had been whispers.

Whispers.

Not a name of who was missing. Not a crime scene. *Whispers.* Was she fucking high? Was I supposed to drop everything for this nonsense?

I fucking well hoped not.

And did they have a shred of proof, evidence, or even so much as a bit of blood spatter? Not that anyone would tell me, and I needed a hell of a lot more to go on than a feeling and errant mutterings of a bunch of gossiping witches.

Witches that sure as shit shouldn't be in Knoxville in the first fucking place. Not after what they'd done. I'd disbanded the Knoxville coven for a reason, and that reason hadn't changed in the three weeks since I'd done it, either.

Shiloh breezed past me to the parlor and plopped her ass on my couch. Well, it wasn't exactly mine, but the Warden house was in my possession for the time being, and possession being nine-tenths of the law, and all that happy horse shit.

"You and I have investigated a lot more together going on a lot less, sweetheart," she sassed, slipping her purse off her shoulder, and setting it on the coffee table with a purpose. The bag clinked with the sound of glass and crystals. Well, it seemed Shiloh wasn't traveling light, then. *Interesting.*

She was right—of course—I had investigated far more going on far less. But that was *before*.

Before almost losing Jay.

Before Bishop.

Before.

I couldn't exactly go back to the "wet behind the ears" girl I was two years ago, nor could I just drop everything because Shiloh had come out of hiding. Though, her risking someone finding out she was actually alive wasn't exactly a small thing, hence the glamour she'd cloaked herself in.

But what more were they going to tell me about the ancient vamp that I didn't already know? Nero's life story was practically burned into my brain, and the atrocities he'd been responsible for made my stomach turn. There was a damn good reason Aemon wanted him dead, and I wasn't too keen on him breathing, either.

And unless they knew shit I didn't, them telling me about whispers just wasn't going to cut it.

"I'm already looking for Nero, Shi," I offered, crossing my arms over my chest. "What more do you want me to do?"

Granted, my sole purpose for looking for the bastard had dried up when Deimos called me off finding his son, but... I needed something other than *not* finding Bishop La Roux to fill my days.

That bit of failure wasn't exactly sitting well with me.

After what Bishop had done, the fact that he was so fucking slippery made me want to bash my head against a wall. And if the ABI wasn't circling the wagons and trying not to go extinct, then I'd have their resources, too.

"I tell you witches are going missing, and you shrug your shoulders, dismissing me? What the fuck happened to you, Darby—other than a bad dye job?" she asked, nodding toward my now-white hair.

First of all, fuck her, and second?

Where would I even start? "Well, let's see. Both my fathers died, my mom tried to rip a hole in the world— you weren't there for that one, but remember me saving your ass? Then, my sister became the new Angel of Death, I got possessed by a Prince of Hell, my boyfriend turned out to be a walking, talking, real-life psychopath who'd been spelling me our entire relationship." I ticked that drama off on my fingers one by one. "There was a zombie horde situation, a wolf war, my house getting blown up, and a god on my front doorstep somewhere in there."

I paused, listening for Tobin and Yazzie, who were

snickering in the kitchen, eavesdropping. "Did I miss anything, Tobin?"

Yes, I can hear you, you nosy shits.

"The best friend getting turned and the brother stuff, I think?" his timid voice called back, reminding me of the bastard of a brother I'd damn near blocked out, and Jay who had transitioned into a half-vamp *whatever*.

My gut dipped and twisted, the memory of almost losing Jay sending my heart into a tailspin.

"And wasn't there a prison stint in there, too?" Yazzie added.

My gaze laser-locked on Shiloh. "I've been busy. And I didn't dye my hair, you twat." I pointed to my hair. "This is what happens when you have hundreds of thousands of souls squirming under your flesh for far too long, and they get ripped out the hard way."

Shiloh's now-pale eyes widened as her expression softened.

Yeah, you fucked up.

"At least you fixed that emotional lock-down issue," Harper muttered, breezing by me to perch on an arm of one of the wingbacks. "I can't feel you at all. Was that a parting gift from Azrael?"

Her words had the breath catching in my lungs, and I fought off the urge to put my blade to her throat.

Breaking my Shiloh stare down, I shot the small

empath a glare. "I realize tact is not your forte, Harper, but maybe *don't* be so flippant about my father's death, mm-kay?"

My heart ached—physically ached—at the loss of both my fathers. Because thoughts of Azrael always turned to Killian, the man who'd raised me. Hell, I still saw the knife flipping end over end every time I closed my eyes.

Jesus, I need therapy. Or a vacation. Probably both.

Maybe it was my tone, maybe it was my hand resting on the dagger at my hip, but Harper's ass barely touched the leather seat before she stood back up, her hands patting the air like she was trying to calm me down.

"I wasn—"

"I don't care." Her apology wasn't necessary or wanted, and I sure as hell didn't want her to stay any longer than she had to. Harper was great, sure, but I was already tapped out on pleasantries for the foreseeable future. The nice part of me—the one that actually gave a fuck about people—was long gone. It was probably stuck under the rubble of the caves, along with my safety, happiness, and my will to fucking live.

"You want me to look for missing witches—witches that shouldn't fucking be here in the first place? Fine. You want me to find Nero? Fine. You want something else? Too fucking bad. I'm tapped out. I'm one person with a small team and you've given me exactly fuck all in the way of information. I need more to go on than 'Witches are missing, and we think it maybe might be this one guy, sorta' to start my investigation."

Dahlia put a gentle hand on my shoulder, the touch making me want to slam my fist in her face. "What happened to you?"

As gently as I could, I plucked her hand off me. I didn't want to hurt her, but I sure as hell didn't want her to touch me, either. "A lot. Now if you need something further or have more information, email Tobin. He'll get me the message."

Was I being rude? Yes.

Should I offer them coffee and a cookie and gab like normal? Also, yes.

But that part of me was broken, and I didn't know if it would ever come back. Maybe I'd be this awful, shriveled husk of the woman I once was forever.

Or maybe I needed more than a week to heal from having my whole world rocked. Again.

"Jaysus, Mary, and Joseph," Hildy remarked, materializing into his solid form in the middle of the room—top hat, cane, and all. "Can't ya take a hint? The lot of ya need to leave."

My ghostly grandfather appearing out of nowhere was not exactly new. Hell, he'd been doing it so much, I quit flinching. To say he'd been doing that a lot recently, would be a fucking understatement. He was acting like he was my own personal Doberman, guarding me against the majority of the world.

It thawed me some—not a lot, but some.

If only I could believe I was safe. Then maybe I could get some damn sleep.

But Bishop La Roux was still at large, Nero was the bogeyman in the background, and the entirety of the Knoxville arcane world was in fucking shambles. Now I had missing witches? Witches that probably held a grudge against me? Witches that likely did not want my help?

Perfect.

Dahlia and Harper didn't so much as flinch at Hildy's sudden appearance—too used to him from our time at the Night Watch—but Shiloh jumped from the couch like she'd been electrocuted. Granted, she knew about Hildy, but a year ago, he hadn't exactly gone the corporeal route.

"Where the hell did you come from?" she hissed, clutching her purse to her chest like he might steal it, her now-auburn bob swinging with the motion.

Hildy narrowed his eyes. "Around, about. Not that it matters to you. I told ya to leave. It's time you got on with that."

Shiloh's new face gained a hurt expression as she shouldered her bag. "It's not like I'm telling you about a stubbed toe, Darby. Witches *are* missing, and it's like you don't even care."

But I did. I did care. I just couldn't drop everything I was already doing.

"Because I won't hop-to immediately? I told you I was already looking for Nero. What more do you want me to do?" I'd already asked that question, but the repeat was necessary. "If I hear anything about the witches, you know I'll act on it, but seriously? You coming here, acting like this? Friends or not, it's complete bullshit."

My gaze moved from Shiloh to Harper to Dahlia. "Sloane would be disappointed in the both of you." My eyes returned to Shiloh. "You wanted the ABI out of Knoxville. Congratulations, they're out. The consequences of that are there are far less people to investigate when bad shit happens. I get it. You expected it to be like it was when we did our shit under the radar, and no one was the wiser. But I'm not the girl I was then, and you can't have it both ways."

Disappointment lined Shiloh's features, the grooves of her new face deepening with each refusal. "I'll rally the witches we have left. See if any of the good ones are still around. Maybe we can start looking for the missing.

And…" She trailed off, casting her gaze downward. "I'm sorry for coming here like this."

I couldn't tell her it was okay because it wasn't. And I sure as hell wouldn't be putting my nose to the ground —not when I had so much more on my plate than I could handle.

The front door opened behind me, straightening my spine, and making me reach for my weapons. I practically dove for cover, slipping behind the parlor wall and using the mirror mounted on the opposite one to see around the corner.

Yeah, I'd modified the décor to make sure there were no more blind spots. So sue me.

Agent Acker breezed through the opening, slamming the door behind him. Well, "breezed" was the wrong word. Marched was more like it, the loud bang of wood cracking against the doorframe, flashing the heat of adrenaline through me.

"Darby?" Acker's wide eyes met mine through the mirror before falling to the gun that had somehow materialized in my hand. I hadn't even remembered pulling it from its holster, nor did I know how the dagger got out of its sheath.

Oops.

"Remember our talk about safe entry points?" I growled, holstering my weapons, trying not to let the embarrassment of me jumping like a feral cat in front of everyone burn me alive. It was bad enough I'd been a rude, angsty bitch to three women I might call my friends, but this?

And I'd sat all three of them down and we'd gone over the entry protocol. *Twice.*

Acker's already-pale face went gray. "Sorry. I-I forgot." His gaze shifted to the three women in the room. He nodded in deference. "Ladies."

His cheeks pinked a little, like he was holding his breath.

"Time to leave, I think," Harper muttered, ushering Shiloh and Dahlia toward the front door. "I'll contact Tobin when we know more, and…" She trailed off for a second, her lips turning down. "I'm sorry about what I said."

The best I could do was offer her a shrug, because saying it was okay would probably fucking kill me.

And worse? I couldn't even stand there and watch them leave. Because as much as I appreciated them being my friends, I just didn't want to look at them one more second. Turning my back to them, I headed back to the kitchen, praying my coffee was still hot. I'd barely taken a sip when Acker and Hildy crowded in behind me, Acker's energy filling the room with "not good" tidings.

Don't scream. Don't scream. Don't scream. Do not yell at the poor agent who is probably just the messenger, Darby. Just breathe.

I set my cup down and took a calming breath. Whatever was about to come out of his mouth was going to irritate me far past my threshold for bullshit. "What is it?"

Acker winced, pressing his lips together so hard the edges turned white. My gut was threatening to eat itself with the sheer level of unease roiling inside it, and he was pussyfooting around?

"Jesus, fuck, Ambrose. Out with it." I snatched my coffee cup off the counter and tossed back the scalding liquid.

"Umm… I got word there was a body found at the National Cemetery." He swallowed, wringing his hands like Tobin sometimes did. "A witch body."

Of *course* there was.

2

The Knoxville National Cemetery was just outside the arcane border within the city proper. And by "just," I meant thirty fucking feet. The arcane world and the human one—at least outside of Haunted Peak—didn't seem to interact too much in this town, the borders warded, and the people smart enough to not let the worlds mix.

That was until a witch had been sacrificed in the middle of a national landmark—or at least that's what Acker had heard.

The Knoxville National Cemetery—like all cemeteries—gave me the creeps, but this one in particular? It screamed ritual death magic in a way I just couldn't stand. First off, the damn thing was one big circle. The drive was a circle, the graves were in concentric circles. In the middle was an obelisk for fuck's sake.

I was all for having a landscaping plan and everything, but this?

This took planning to a whole other level and made me wonder what arcaner designed the damn thing. Because no way would this level of sacred geometry be an accident—especially since it was situated right over a fucking ley line.

Gritting my teeth, I surveyed the circle and the swarm of buzzing cops. Mostly male, mostly uniform, they seemed to be for crowd control more than anything else. Not that there was a crowd too big for them to manage. Granted, I didn't notice any press lurking about, so at least there was that.

Yazzie and Acker trailed behind me as I picked my way over cracked cement, the walkway leading to the center monument a ruined wreck. And it wasn't just from time or weather, either. No, part of the walkway had barely survived whatever magic had been released here, the smoldering rock still steaming.

The odor of spent magic, burning earth, and blood filled the air, along with the early summer honeysuckle and pine—the odd dichotomy less than pleasant.

The call of a soul beckoned me forward, its peculiar, buzzing demand ringing in my ears like a gong. And I relented, picking my way forward until a uniform barred my way, leaving me stuck in the amorphous crowd with too many strangers.

"I'm going to need you to step back, ma'am," a uniform barked, crossing his arms over his chest, and my eye actually twitched when I recognized the man.

It was the same damn cop that had tried to shoo me away from the Dubois nest fire.

"Oh, great. You again," Yazzie muttered, pulling his fake FBI badge. I wasn't quite sure how the FBI and ABI did business or what agreement—if any—they had, but Yazzie waved that badge around like it was real.

Hell, maybe it was.

The cop briefly glanced at the shield before returning his gaze to me. Unlike the Dubois nest fire, it was broad daylight, the late spring evening shying away in favor of the sticky heat. But in the light—or rather with new eyes —I studied the man.

Dark hair cropped close to his head barely hid the streak of gray at his temple. Smile—or squint—lines fanned out from his green eyes, the unkind orbs filled with disgust or disdain, I couldn't tell which. He was tall enough—at about my height—and seemed in good enough shape. Though, if he was in his late thirties or forties and still in a uniform, he'd damn well have to be to keep up with the rookies.

Before, I hadn't bothered to get his name, but now, my gaze drifted to the brass nameplate pinned to his navy uniform shirt. The name "N. Preston" didn't ring any bells for me, but that didn't mean much.

Hooking a finger in the bridge of my sunglasses, I pinned him with a cold glare. "Tell me—is it fibbies in general, my gender, or me in particular you don't like, Preston? Because this is the second time in a matter of days that you have skirted around another agent to tell me to get off a crime scene, and I gotta say, it's pissing me off."

A sneer curled his lip as he planted his feet, leaning forward just a touch too close for my comfort. "Maybe I don't like your kind, *Warden*," he growled, cutting through any and all levels of pretense. "Maybe I don't like trying to clean up arcane fuck-shit on my only day off. *Maybe I—*"

I caught sight of his KPD brethren stopping to stare and cut him off. "Shut. Up," I growled, fighting off the urge to cover his mouth with my hand. The absolute last thing I needed was a cranky beat cop exposing the arcane world to all and fucking sundry. "If you know who I am and even an inkling of what's good for you, you will keep your fucking mouth shut until I tell you to open it."

Snatching my cell from my back pocket, I dialed Tobin's number.

"Yeah, boss?" he answered, the timid waver to his voice gone now that he was alone in the house and couldn't see my face. Tobin didn't like direct contact of any kind, but on the phone? In front of a computer? He was an absolute powerhouse.

"I need everything you have on an Officer N. Preston." I squinted at the shield pinned to his chest. "Badge number 745632. And I need it yesterday, if you please."

Tobin paused briefly, a faint snicker rattling down the line. Tobin loved it when other people were in trouble. His keyboard clacking like machine gun fire was music to my ears. "On it. Give me five."

Without so much as a nod to polite phone etiquette, the line disconnected, and I stuffed the cell back in my pocket. I'd have to talk to him about that.

Staring at the prick whose face had turned an unhealthy shade of puce in the short time I was on the phone, I tilted my head to the side and narrowed my eyes.

"Now that's done—what were you saying about my kind again? Not that you know what my kind even *is* or what I'm capable of." The subtle buzz around the guy had a solid human flavor to it, but I'd been wrong before.

I'd been wrong about a lot of things.

"Cat got your tongue?" I prompted when Preston remained silent. "Maybe you have something you want to tell me before my guy comes back with every speck of dirt you have in your life? Every footprint you've left in the sand, every wrong you've ever done. Anything?" I quirked a clearly irritated brow. "No?"

Preston ground his teeth, not backing down an inch. "This is the third one of these *this week*." He hiked a thumb behind him to the monument where most of the officers were clustered. "I don't need to keep cleaning up witch shit, Warden. This keeps up, and I'll stop."

His words had my whole body going cold. "Third one of *what* this week?"

Preston's eyes widened like I'd caught him off guard. "W-witch murders," he breathed, finally grasping the gravity of the situation. "The first two were easy to cover up, but this one—"

Fire burned in my gaze as I slowly pivoted on a heel to stare at Acker. His face went gray as he shook his head. "First I'm hearing of it."

My head whipped to Yazzie. "Don't look at me. I've been on wolf detail and patrol."

Yazzie had taken point on keeping the grounds safe

for us. After the last attack—and subsequent death toll —he'd gotten about as much sleep as I had for the last few days.

Massaging my temple, I returned my focus on the increasingly agitated cop barring my way. "Who have you notified about these deaths? I take it I am not your first brush with my kind, so, who is your point person?"

Preston stepped back, shock graying his skin. "Th- the council. I talked to Astrid Byrne directly. She's the wi—"

I held up a hand. No need for him to give me the full title of the witch bitch pulling his strings, I knew *exactly* who his point person was. Pulling a card from my messenger bag, I handed it to him.

"Next time you have anything hinky come across your desk, give me a call instead. Cut out the middleman, as it were, since there seems to be a hiccup in me getting the message." When he hesitantly took my card, I added, "You shouldn't have to be cleaning up any arcane messes. I'm sorry you had to stick your neck out like that."

His shoulders drooped a little, his expression lightening. "You aren't like she said."

Huffing a dispirited laugh, I asked, "Astrid? Well, she doesn't like me much. It probably has something to do with how little I give a shit about what she thinks. But that's not your problem."

He nodded, scratching at the stubble on his jaw. "If I see anything, I'll give you a call."

I managed a smile—it was fake and hollow, but I did it. "I'd appreciate it."

What in the absolute blue fuck was going on here? Shiloh had said witch abductions—*maybe*—not a damn thing about witch *murders*. Why had Astrid not told anyone about this? How was she keeping it quiet?

And what else had she been keeping from me?

Perfect. Just fucking perfect. As if I didn't already have enough on my plate.

Sliding past Preston, I shot Acker a glare, communicating every ounce of my displeasure.

"I'll make a call," he muttered, fishing his phone out of his pocket. It made me wonder how he'd heard of this particular murder and what made it so damn different.

Half of my questions were answered as soon as I weaved through the throng of cops to the center cordoned-off square of the monument.

A very dead woman was tied to the stone with what appeared to be barbed wire, the rusted metal obviously pressed into her skin while she was still alive. It wrapped around her wrists, pulling them wide as it circled the large obelisk before trussing her up at her ankles.

Streams of blood pooled at her feet, staining the stone and her light-pink flats red. Her head hung forward, her dark hair curtaining her features. I had a feeling I didn't want to look at her face—especially since her skin was a mottled mess.

Death masks were never pretty, but this one would be especially haunting. Spell ingredients littered the ground at her feet, including a banana python—sans head—and bowls full of blood, and jars of varying shapes and sizes filled to the brim with keys. It was the keys that struck me. Keys had a purpose. Sometimes they were offerings, sometimes they were for opening portals, and sometimes they were for dark things.

Summoning things.

Sigils had been carved into the ground—what was left of it—their edges and meanings lost to the rubble, the monument itself, and the victim's skin.

Sigils I didn't recognize.

Great.

"Thank Christ they called in the Feds," a man said to my left, yanking my gaze from the dead body. "I thought we were gonna have to deal with this bullshit on our own."

He was tall and barrel-chested, the aging detective

offering his absolute trashcan lid of a hand. "Ron Herndon, Homicide."

When I didn't take his hand, Yazzie offered his. "I'm Agent Yazzie and this is SSA Adler. The blond guy on the phone is Agent Acker." Acker raised his head at his name and gave the detective a nod before returning to his call.

SSA stood for Senior Special Agent—a title I did not have nor want, but it offered a bit of deference to the absolute bullshit "Warden" position I held.

Herndon seemed appeased at Yazzie's introductions, though his gaze was cool when it fell on me. I'd really have to get over that no-touch thing sometime soon. It was pissing people off.

"Give me a rundown of what you've got," I said, moving my gaze from him back to the scene. "Please."

I tacked on that "please" so I didn't seem like a total bitch. We'd need this guy's help at some point, and burning bridges seemed like a bad way to go if I was going to be Warden for any length of time.

"We got an anonymous tip at about five p.m. saying there was a dead body here. Unit responded approximately seven minutes later. Whole place was smoking, cracked cement and all, like a damn bomb had gone off. The officer checked the woman's pulse but couldn't find one. Then he called it in, cordoned off the area, and here we are. We're still waiting on the ME, but the scene photographer has gotten all he needs, so…"

Nodding, I ignored the trickle of sweat skating down my spine and shifted my gaze back to the detective. "Very good. Thank you. If you don't mind, could you have the photographer send the images to us? Yazzie will give you the info."

"S-sure," he muttered, seemingly confused at my direct question. I couldn't blame him. I'd dealt with Feds before, and I did not and would not treat him the same as I had been. "You got any theories, Agent? Things like this just don't happen he—"

"Yes, they do," I said, cutting him off. "Plenty of people are killed every day in this city. And there are plenty of people looking for their fifteen minutes of fame. But my theory? Someone wanted to make a spectacle. Why else call it in?"

Whoever it was, they wanted us here, staring at a tortured woman on a ruined cemetery full of desecrated dead. The only good thing I could say about it was at least the graves were intact. The last thing I needed was evidence of a death mage in the middle of this mess.

My nerves were bad enough already.

Because on top of the dead woman, and dead snake, and jars of keys, there was something else mighty amiss here. Not all cemeteries were full of ghosts, however, the newer the cemetery, the likelier ghosts would be hanging around. This one wasn't new—especially the graves closest to the monument.

Those were over a hundred years old, the ghosts long since moved on.

The problem was that there were *no* ghosts.

Anywhere.

Especially not anywhere near the very fresh, very dead woman.

3

Missing Jay and Jimmy never hit me more than it did right then. There was nothing wrong with Yazzie or Acker exactly, but Jay's presence at a crime scene added a level of safety that I just didn't have here.

An overwhelming weight settled in my gut. There would never be a time where I just rolled out of bed and opened the door for Jay calling me to a scene. He wouldn't tattle on me to Dad anymore. He wouldn't sass me for scaring the rookies.

Everything was different now, and as someone who'd had her whole life rocked about five times too many, well, it just sucked.

Slipping booties on my feet, I steeled my spine and clenched my jaw. Jay was alive. Jimmy was safe. Sarina…

was a little broken, but she had her eyes open, and Uncle Dave was an alpha now. Yeah, we were all a little fucked up. Yeah, we'd suffered some losses.

But we were here and breathing, and that meant something.

Didn't it?

Ignoring the still-constant buzz of a soul calling to me, I ducked under the police tape. It didn't make a lick of sense. I couldn't see a single soul in this damn cemetery, but there was one. I just knew it. Wriggling my hands into gloves, I moved to inspect the body.

"Anyone look in her pockets for identification or find a purse anywhere?"

The added weight of gloves in this heat had me praying for a cool breeze of some kind. I'd never regretted wearing a leather jacket so much in my entire life. But something had to hide the boatload of weapons I had strapped to my body, and the blazer just wouldn't do the job.

Were they overkill? Maybe.

But I wouldn't be going anywhere ever again without a fucking arsenal, and that was just how it had to be.

Herndon smartly remained on the other side of the line—a welcome quality in a man. It had taken three years of pranks to teach Sal that much, and he still forgot on occasion. "No, ma'am, we did not. But no one has looked yet. Most of my guys are a little creeped out by the locale, if you know what I'm saying."

Oh, he doesn't want to search a cemetery? Neither do I, pal.

Shrugging, I reached to gently lift the curtain of hair away from the victim's face, not bothering to turn around. "Do you think you could talk to the first officer on scene and see if ya'll can look around for a purse of some kind? I don't think you'll find one, but it can't hurt to look."

I needed him somewhere—anywhere—but here while I processed this body, and if sending him on a wild goose chase was my only option other than telling him to "shoo," well, then, so be it. When he didn't say anything, I dropped the victim's hair and shot him a look that let him know my question was not a question.

It was an order.

Herndon let out a gust of air so powerful it practically whistled. "Sure thing."

When he peeled off—thankfully taking most of his buddies with him—I finally looked at Yazzie who was also on the outside of the line. "What do you smell?"

There were a lot of benefits to having a shifter on the team. One of them being the awesome nose. Plus, Yazzie seemed like a nice enough guy. I didn't get an ick feeling from him, anyway. Granted, my opinion on anyone was suspect—probably until the end of time—after the

Bishop bullshit. I didn't know if I could ever trust myself again.

Then again, I did have Jimmy's necklace on. No one could spell me anymore. No one could use me like a puppet to get whatever they wanted.

No one could—

I shook my head, trying to get rid of the awful thoughts and images that had been swirling there for days.

"Witch magic, death magic, and dead witch." He pinched his brow, shaking his head. "And blood. Too much from just one person. It doesn't make any sense. It's all from her, but there's more than thirty units here. It's like…" He trailed off, but I picked up the thread.

Staring at the blood staining her clothes, the monument, and the amount pooled at her feet, I got the message just fine. "It's like someone bled her, healed her, and bled her all over again?"

Yazzie yanked his head up, staring at me like he'd never seen me before now. "You've seen shit like this before?"

Lifting a shoulder in chagrin, I returned my attention to the victim. "Once, but never like this."

Four years ago, Shiloh had me looking into a body sort of like this one, only the blood hadn't been spilled all over everything. It had been in bags—too many bags for just one person to give in the scant time the witch had been abducted. Later, we found out it had been a vampire bleeding the witch dry, healing her, and then bleeding her all over again.

That time it had been rogue members of the Dubois nest trying to run a doped-up blood ring, and there sure as hell hadn't been witch magic involved.

Just witch blood.

And this time all the blood was spoiled, not saved, which had me thinking, it might not be a vamp at all. No vampire would waste this much blood.

Gathering myself, I gently lifted the matted strands of hair away from her face again and tilted up her chin. Her skin was mottled, yet deathly pale, the faint traces of blood still in her system, pooling in her cheeks by sheer force of gravity. Slashes of dark eyebrows cut across her forehead, seemingly darker now that she'd been drained. High cheekbones and a full mouth, she'd been beautiful in her living days.

Unfortunately, the witch's features weren't familiar, so identifying her and letting her people know she was gone would be off the table.

The former members of the Knoxville coven's faces were still burned into my brain, their treachery and betrayal enough to keep every single name in my head. But this witch hadn't been there the day my father died.

"You recognize her?" I asked, turning the woman's face to Yazzie.

"Can't say I do," he rumbled, barely glancing at the witch's features before looking anywhere else.

I got it. Not everyone was around death as much as I'd been. Not everyone could look at a body and still see the living, breathing person they used to be. Granted, I was usually staring at their ghosts while I did that, but it felt the same.

As gently as I could, I returned her to her resting hang. It seemed disrespectful, considering how she'd been killed, but until the ME got here, there was little else I could do. Mincing over pools of blood, I ducked back under the tape and removed my gloves and booties.

As horrific as it was, it felt normal—for once—to be at a scene. To be searching for clues, to be investigating something. It was a chance to do some good in the world again. Not that overthrowing evil wolf alpha dictators or stopping a vamp-wolf war in its tracks wasn't awesome or anything, but it wasn't the same.

It was too big, too reaching. And for all the world—at least right now—I wanted to be small. I wanted to be a tiny cog in a big wheel that I didn't have to turn myself.

A flash of gray caught my eye as I was stuffing my soiled booties in a biohazard bag. At first, I'd figured it was Hildy, shadowing me like he had been for the last two days. But the specter flickered in a worrying way that had my teeth on edge and my hand on my gun.

Black hair hanging over her face, the ghost flashed in and out of view, her wounds weeping silvery blood.

I slapped the back of my hand against Yazzie's arm, not taking my gaze off the soon-to-be-turning specter. "I need you to call a 'Code Boo' and I need you to do it now."

Yazzie chuckled much like Bishop had when I'd used that phrase and the memory had me fighting the urge to draw my gun. "Wha—"

"Remember Linus and the wolves?" I barked, cutting him off. "We have one of those situations. In. Public. Clear everyone out. Now. Call in a bomb threat or something."

In all honesty, I didn't give a shit what he did as long as he got everyone out of here, and now.

I vaguely heard Yazzie bark orders at the milling officers while I carefully approached the flickering ghost, who was clawing at her throat and face, a silent scream pulling at her distorted lips.

"It's okay," I cooed, not bothering to hide my obvious "speaking to the dead" routine. We didn't have time for pretense right now. "You're okay."

Slowly, I reached out a hand, calling her to me in my mind. But like many poltergeists, she had a will of her own that was far stronger than I was. She flickered solid for a second before going gray again, the subtle *pop* of her turning drowned out by a wail screeching up her throat.

Her form faded a bit, becoming even more see-through, and I hated to say, I lunged. My little pea brain figured that if I touched her, not only could I save the very living populace from a poltergeist, but I could also find out who she was and what happened to her.

But my lunge ended with me going ass over tea kettle in the dirt, as not only my hand but my whole fucking body passed right through her. Maybe it was the adrenaline, maybe it was Azrael's gift—whatever the fuck that was—but I was up and on my feet in an instant, the screaming smart to my hip barely registering.

Maybe it was the fact that I passed through a poltergeist instead of absorbing it. Yeah, that was definitely it.

The woman flickered again, turning solid for another long moment before graying out. Every time she went solid, her scream got louder, piercing my ears with the screeching wail.

Sloane? Babe? I'm gonna need you to grab your girl here. This is above my pay grade.

A nervous laugh bubbled up my throat as I stared at

the woman. What the fuck else was I supposed to do while I waited for my sister to come save my ass?

I could try talking to her again.

Sure. My gaze skittered to all the cops leaving the area. It was possible I could talk to a ghost in broad daylight with a bunch of human civilians looking on.

Absolutely.

No problem.

Fuck.

"Hey, can you tell me your name?" *Lame, Darby. Lame.* "Can you say anything?"

The specter seemed agitated—*no, shit*—her see-through body sweeping the grass in great jerks of movement. Every few seconds her body would go solid, the silvery blood at her wrists and ankles shifting to scarlet in the light before flickering back to gray again.

"My name is Darby and I'm going to find out who did this to you," I babbled, trying to think of something—anything—to say to this woman who'd been tortured right up until her last breath. "Would you like to rest? If you come to me, I can send you someplace nice?"

That was iffy at best. The last time I'd tried to touch her, I hadn't been successful, but that didn't mean that I *couldn't* send her on. One try didn't mean anything.

Right?

The sigils on her arms began to glow with silvery

light, and when she flickered back solid, her screams got even louder. The sigils burned like embers in her skin, so bright it had me shielding my eyes and backing away. I didn't know how to help her. I didn't know if I could.

Sloane Emerson Cabot, get your ass up here now and help me with this shit.

But she didn't come, at least not before the ghost's entire form started glowing, not just the sigils. Before I knew it, an arm hooked my middle and I was up and over a shoulder, staring at a decent jean-clad backside, as whoever it was hauled ass away from the screaming, glowing specter.

A few moments later, I was dumped on the asphalt behind a black-and-white, the screams so loud I thought my eardrums would burst. Then the whole world rocked, glass blowing out from the unit's windows, tires blowing, the ground cracking and all.

My ears felt like they were going to explode, the intense ringing rattling my head as warm, sticky wetness dripped from my nose. Gritty asphalt and glass cut into my hands as I pushed myself to standing, the world swirling around me. My gaze was immediately pulled to the monument. The ghost was long gone, leaving behind a crater the size of Texas that had taken *out* the memorial, the body, and every stitch of evidence there was to be had.

This was bad. Very, very bad. But I couldn't quite pinpoint exactly what was bad.

You have a concussion, stupid. Sit down.

My stomach lurched as the world tilted, and I rested my hip against the black-and-white for support. Before I could get my footing, a hard hand latched onto my shoulder and whirled me around. The world spun a little further than intended, but my wobbly vision finally snagged on my favorite council member in all her redheaded glory as she shoved her fingers in my face, yelling her stupid head off.

Astrid Byrne had been a pain in my ass since she tried to throw me under the bus what seemed like ages ago. In reality, it had been more like a week, but I'd seen some shit since then. Roughly, I shrugged off her hand, reaching up to my ears. I couldn't hear a word she was saying, and that made a hell of a lot more sense when my fingers came away red.

That blast had rocked my shit, and Astrid was busy jumping up and down on my last nerve.

Her garbled voice got louder—if not clearer—and she shoved my shoulder, her pale skin going red as she screamed in my face. Yazzie tried to get in between us, but Astrid shoved him away, too, adding a little witchy *oomph* into her shove.

Okay, shoving my shoulder was one thing, but using her powers on one of my guys?

Hell.

No.

Anger had my footing on more solid ground. "Bitch, I can't hear a word you're saying, but if you touch one of us again, I'll lay you the *fuck* out. And I really don't give a *shit* if you *are* a councilmember."

Her face twisted, the sneer curling her lip as she made a threat severe enough to have Yazzie and Acker's expressions going white. Then she planted both her hands into my chest and shoved, her power skating right over me, thanks to Jimmy's necklace.

I stumbled back a step as a red haze blanketed my vision. I could have been bleeding from the eyes or—and this was far more likely—I was just done with her shit.

Before she could snap off another bullshit retort—one I still couldn't fucking hear, by the way—I hauled back and punched her right in the face. Granted, I pulled the punch just a smidge right before it made contact so I wouldn't cave in her skull, but she still dropped like a stone, knocked out cold.

No one put their fucking hands on me. Not ever again.

The crowd of cops, along with Yazzie and Acker, stood with mouths agape as I stepped over Astrid like she was a piece of trash on the sidewalk. "I'm going to see Ingrid. Ya'll finish up here?"

Without so much as a nod, I headed for my Jeep.

Nods were bad. Nods would make me throw up.

But I was making the exit, dammit.

Even if it killed me.

4

My Jeep appeared to survive the ghost bombing, faring far better than I had, the big red beauty a beacon for my shuffling. All I needed was a seat and some air-conditioning, and maybe some food, and I'd heal right up.

Sure.

My ringing ears and bloody nose most likely attested to the exact opposite, but whatever.

I was going to Ingrid's, and I was going to see Jay and everything else could quite literally fuck all the way off.

"Jaysus, Mary, and Joseph," Hildy muttered, his thick Irish accent an indicator of just how pissed he was. Good of him to show up when it was all over. "I leave ya for ten minutes and look at ya."

Rolling my eyes made the whole world spin cockeyed for a second, and I pinched the bridge of my nose to stem the zap to my brain. "I've already knocked the living shit out of one person today, Hildenbrand. You want to make it two?"

My grandfather chuckled. "Is that how we're treatin' our elders now, lass? And here I was ready and willin' to heal you all up."

The fact that I couldn't hear shit else proved that the grave talker magic—and just death magic, besides—had me hearing ghosts *inside* my head and not with my ears. And I decided to focus on that revelation rather than actually sock Hildy right in his smug face.

Tiredly, I opened the door to my Jeep and dumped myself into the driver's seat. Naturally, Hildy appeared right beside me like we were going on a trip or something. My fingers felt for the "Start" button, and two seconds later, blissful air-conditioning caressed my skin.

"I don't really care if you heal me or not," I croaked, leaning my head back on the head rest. "I want to know what just happened. Why did that ghost explode like a damn bomb?"

Okay, so I cared if he healed me a little bit. My head was really starting to hurt, and the ringing sound was getting on my nerves. Also, my tummy was threatening to toss up all the food I'd eaten in the last week if my head didn't stop spinning. I cared a lot.

Hildy latched a hand on my arm, lending me a little of his power. I still wasn't in tip-top shape, but I didn't want to chuff on my boots anymore, so solid win.

"What do you mean a ghost exploded?" he asked, his voice as cold as ice. Both Hildy's and his cane's eyes began to glow green, his body going solid.

I gestured to the smoking, Texas-sized crater in the middle of the cemetery. "What the fuck do you think I mean? A. Ghost. Exploded. And I tried, okay? I tried absorbing her. I tried calling to her. I tried talking her down. Then some sigils carved into her arms started glowing and then she start—"

Hildy's grip got tighter. "What sigils?"

I wrenched my wrist from his hold, rubbing at the sore spot. "I have no idea. Never seen them before. The scene photographer had been through already, though, so maybe we'll get to see them."

At least, I hoped we would. If they didn't show up on the photo, we would be up shit creek. And considering those photos were the only thing we had by way of evidence, well…

"Did you ever stop to consider that you were the target?" Hildy seethed through gritted teeth. "Did you ever think that the bomb was meant to kill you?"

Yanking my phone from my pocket, I was ecstatic to find it still worked, and I dialed Tobin again. No, I actually hadn't thought of that. And I really, really didn't want to.

"Yeah, boss?"

"New priority over the Preston deep dive. Get the crime scene photos from the photographer and send them to me. Please."

"On it." And then he hung up on me. No "Goodbye," no "Is there anything else," just a click of the call being disconnected. I'd really have to talk to him about that.

Gritting my teeth, I put my car into "Drive."

Someone wants to kill me. What else is new?

Walking into a vampire nest covered in blood was not the best way to stay breathing—especially if you were visiting a newly turned vampire. In the car, I mopped up my face as much as I could, with a very sullen Hildy looking on.

"You won't even talk to me about this, lass?" he asked, appearing right next to me as I yanked my arms out of my jacket.

Blood stained my black *Green Day* shirt, soaking through the tank top beneath. *Great.*

"What's there to talk about?" I grumbled, shoving my car door open and moving to the hatchback. There had to be a fresh shirt back there somewhere. "Someone is fucking with the very laws of nature, murdering witches, and trying to kill me. *Whoop-de-do*. And *tomorrow* the sun will come up and the world will spin."

It was a testament to my lack of "give a fuck" that I yanked on the first shirt I saw, not really caring that I was changing my clothes in broad daylight.

In public.

I would *not* be walking in to see Jay when I was covered in blood. I just wouldn't. Hard. Pass.

Okay, so the "public" thing was a stretch. I was parked at the rear drive of Björn's—or maybe Ingrid's—estate up in Beacon Hills. I couldn't really be sure who owned the place, but there was enough tree cover that no neighbor would spot me. The presence of cameras literally everywhere, though, made my temper tantrum less than private.

Shrugging on my weapons and jacket, I continued ignoring Hildy. I was really getting tired of this shit. Why did people just *love* killing each other? Why did I always have a target on my back?

And why couldn't it stop for one fucking day so I could rest?

Just. One. Fucking. Day.

Was that too much to ask?

Apparently.

The side door to the garage opened, and my best

friend appeared in the doorway as I slipped my arms back into my jacket.

Jeremiah Cooper was a tall man at six foot two, with the build of a pro-quarterback. His jaw was chiseled, his skin tanned, and even though he'd been turned into a vampire, his eyes were still the crystalline blue they'd been when we were children.

The only difference between the boy he'd been then and who he was now was the faint tracery of scars that webbed over his neck where he'd been attacked by a reanimated wolf. Bishop's handiwork was bright against the tan of his skin, reminding me of just how stupid I'd been to trust the death mage.

Just how much I'd been duped.

Just how much I'd believed in the goodness of people.

"About time you showed up," he called, striding right out into the waning sunlight. "I thought I was going to have to stage a jailbreak and come find you."

Real vampires—unlike in fiction—had no problems walking in the sun. Yes, they were nocturnal, and yes, they drank blood, but the sun was not their enemy. Neither was holy water, garlic, or silver, though, a stake to the heart would kill just about anyone.

"Sorry," I mumbled, hesitating before moving forward. It had been two days since I made it over here.

Two days of worrying about his transition and if he was okay. Granted, most of that time had been spent flipping off the council and tattling on Bishop, but that really wasn't an excuse.

Honestly? I was scared.

That he blamed me.

That he hated me.

That he would want nothing to do with me now that his old life was gone.

"You about done with your pity party? This self-flagellation you're doing is tired, babe." Jay tapped the tip of his nose. "You reek of guilt and sadness. And blood. What have you been doing?"

I rolled my eyes—which didn't hurt this time—and opened my arms wide for a hug. I hadn't hugged Jay when he woke up. Being covered in zombie guts— three days post-battle—had me at peak-reek levels. No one should be subjected to a stank hug. That was just rude.

But he didn't leave me hanging. Jay moved *fast-fast*, wrapping me in a hug so tight I thought one of my ribs would break. I didn't care. His flesh was still warm, and he still smelled the same, and he was alive.

Jay was alive.

A moment later, my arms wrapped around him, the sheer relief bringing tears to my eyes as I hugged my best friend in the entire world, and thanked all the deities I knew of that he was still with me.

Call me selfish all you want to, but I'd take vampire-Jay over no Jay any day of the week and twice on Sundays.

"Shh," he murmured, steadying me when my knees threatened to give out. "I'm not going anywhere, D. I'm here to stay."

Jay was more durable now than he had been when he'd been human. He was faster, stronger. He would live forever if he could swing it. It was safe to be around him now. It was safe.

"What's all this?" Jimmy called, and I peeled my head from Jay's shoulder.

The giant Viking-looking elf had also grown up with us, his long blond hair covering the pointed ears that heralded his lineage. Granted, when we'd been children, Jimmy had been the skinny, short waiflike boy we'd needed to protect. Not so much now.

Gently, I pushed out of Jay's arms, standing on my own two feet, like an adult and everything. "Just having a breakdown, Jim. Nothing to worry about."

He nodded like he'd done the same over the last couple of days. "Sounds about right. Though, it looks like you've been put through the wringer. Come inside.

Björn makes a mean pancake. You can tell us why you have blood in your ears over breakfast."

At the mere mention of food, my stomach took the opportunity to yowl like a cat in heat. Good to know at least some of my basic functions were still there. Too bad sleep wasn't one of them.

Ten minutes later, I was at a round table in a room I could only call a solarium, if the sheer number of plants and vines curtaining the wide windows were any indication. In front of me were platters of bacon, pancakes, eggs, and a bowl of mixed fruit so big it could be called a vat.

Jay, Jimmy, Björn, and Ingrid sat along with myself and Hildy, my ghostly grandfather staying solid enough to procure himself a seat before winking back to his normal grayed-out form. No one but me was reaching for food, everyone smartly getting the hell out of my way as I loaded up my plate.

"You eat like the *Cookie Monster*," Björn remarked as I stuffed a whole-ass pancake into my mouth. No butter, no compote. No nothing. Just a pancake as big as my head, puffing my cheeks wide.

"It's an endearing quality once you get used to it," Jay replied for me, though his tone suggested otherwise. "As long as she gets food, no one gets hurt. Plus, who wants to deal with getting shot? I know I don't."

Okay, so I was a cranky beast with no social skills when I was hungry. And yeah, so I was *maybe* a certified bitch when I missed meals. But with the ghost at my left literally draining my energy every second he was around me, it wasn't like I could stop.

Swallowing the bite, I reached for my coffee, feigning the manners my father had taught me. "The food is delicious. Thank you so much for having me."

Björn rubbed at his bald head, seemingly appeased at my gratitude, and I took that as my cue that I could continue stuffing my face. After five minutes, I had decimated half the pancakes and bacon, and was working on a full bowl of fruit. The aches in my body were waning, and for the first time all day, hunger wasn't clawing at my belly.

"We need to tell those boys to feed you more, lass," Hildy muttered, his gaze boring a hole in the side of my face. "You're losing too much weight. Bet I could blow ya over with a stiff wind. Ya need to be takin' care of yerself. Ya don't have to earn rest or food or sleep. That's not how this works."

Gritting my teeth, I stabbed a strawberry with my fork. There were only so many hours in the day, and only so much I could handle. I needed more help, but I didn't know how to ask.

"Enough of this shit," Ingrid barked. "You've eaten

enough. Why is there blood in your ears and nose, why is your grandfather hovering over you like a literal shadow, and why—not that I'm complaining—did you lay Astrid out? She called by the way. You broke her jaw."

The smile that curled my lips was satisfaction personified. I munched on my strawberry, positively beaming.

"Well, I laid Astrid out because she shoved me and tried to use magic on me," I answered her before shooting a thankful look at Jimmy. "And that was *after* she pushed my guys. It didn't work out so well for her—whatever she was trying to do."

"That necklace only blocks harmful magic," Jimmy growled. "I tuned it that way so someone could heal your accident-prone ass. Whatever she was trying would have hurt you."

Just like I'd thought. "And I have blood in my ears and nose because a ghost exploded in the middle of the Knoxville National Cemetery and blew out my eardrums."

Ingrid's spine went rigid, but I held up a finger to halt her outburst until I was done.

"And that was *after* a witch got trussed up on the monument with barbed wire and bled to death before going full monkey shit poltergeist. One I could not calm, absorb, or send on." I nodded, sipping my coffee. "And this is the third such witch death this week. Wanna know how many Astrid knew about? Wanna guess how many she kept from me?"

The dark chuckle that bubbled up my throat scared even me. "FYI, Shiloh's back in town. She says witches are missing. I think we found some of them, yeah?"

Ingrid hopped from her seat, pressing her small palms into the table as her eyes went blood-red, her tiny needlelike fangs snapping over her regular teeth.

"I'm going to fucking *kill* that bitch."

5

There was no part of my brain that forgot that Ingrid Dubois was a predator. No single section that looked at her and thought she was anything other than a compact killing machine.

But she was a master of disguise, fooling even the smartest foe with her cherubic cheeks and blonde pigtails.

"Calm down, wee one. No need to go flyin' off the handle just yet," Hildy said, appearing in his seat once more and scaring the living—or rather *undead*—shit out of Björn. "There's more information that Darby just glossed over."

Yeah, I didn't want to get into *that* part just yet. I shot a glare at Hildy as I stuffed a piece of bacon in my mouth.

"Darby," Ingrid growled. "Spill it."

"Fine," I said around the salty bit of goodness. "The witch was clearly the center of a ritual. One where she had been bled about three times as much as a body could hold. There were sigils carved into her arms and the ground, ones I really hope are on the crime scene photos, because the entire area has been reduced to rubble."

Ingrid's face grew paler than her usual alabaster pallor as she planted her ass back on her seat. "Was she—"

"Bled, healed, and bled again? Yeah. Looks like it." I popped another piece of bacon in my mouth, more for something to do than anything else. She needed time to process that a vamp might be involved. Maybe more than one. Plus, with Shiloh coming back to town and trying to blame everything on Nero...

"Tobin should have the pictures any minute now so we can narrow down what was done to the witch. Also? There's a human cop that has been feeding info to Astrid. He said this was the third murder he's covered up *this week*. That's a problem, Ing."

It was one thing for Jay to be my best friend in the known universe and let him in on the arcane world. There were plenty of humans who did know—wives, husbands, close family. But it was a whole other ball of wax for a council member to be keeping a human cop on retainer.

A human cop that was covering up murders. Not only did that grate on my nerves as Warden, but the homicide detective in me wanted to scream. How in the blue fuck was I going to find out anything if Astrid was keeping secrets? And trusting a human cop to keep a lid on everything?

Someone was breaking all the rules, wasn't she?

Ingrid's eye twitched. "I'll have to call Lise." She let out a guttural groan, clearly irritated to have to deal with the new leader of the council. "Fuck, I hate talking to that woman. It makes me almost wish Horace hadn't been such a corrupt, soul-sucking dick cheese. At least he was easier to boss around."

Considering the first and last time I'd met Horace, he'd tried to kill me, I couldn't exactly agree with her. Granted, she'd been the one to rip his head off to save me, so there was that.

"Get the photos. I'll call Lise," she grumbled, stomping off to who knew where to make her phone call.

"You need backup," Jay insisted, pulling my gaze to him. "No way should you be out in the wild—not with everything that has been going on. And now we have who knows who spelling the dead?" He shook his head, rising so fast from his seat that his chair tipped over backward. "No. I'm not letting you do this shit by yourself."

He'd said that before. The same damn day he'd gotten those scars on his neck. "Are you ready? Usually fledglings need a year fo—"

He banged his fists on the table. "Don't give me that shit. I'm barely a vampire to begin with," Jay hissed through elongated fangs so different from Ingrid's. Where hers were a needlelike second set of teeth, his were just sharpened, longer versions of his canines. "See?"

Instead of answering Jay, I stared at his maker, Björn. Jay had eaten regular food like I had. He drank coffee and juice. He hugged me without issue and sat right next to me even though—*apparently*—I still had blood in my ears.

It gave me hope but not much.

"Is he really ready to leave the nest? After two days?" I asked, flicking Jay on the arm when he tried to squawk a protest. "I'm not asking you. I'm asking the man who'll be held responsible if you decide to lose your mind and kill someone. Fledglings are given a *year* to be presented to the queen. If they can't pass her test, they die. If they hurt a human, kill an innocent, or expose the race, the maker *and* the fledgling dies."

Christ on toast, he was being a stubborn brat about this shit, and it was serious. He was only alive because of Björn's help. He was only here because Björn allowed him to be. My best friend in the world was only breathing because Björn had taken on a progeny of his own.

Jay crossed his arms, glaring at me like I was telling him something he knew already. Maybe he did know, maybe he didn't, but his petulant attitude was getting us nowhere.

"What if you're not ready, and you kill someone, huh? What if you expose the arcane world to humans— humans who are all too ready to kill each other, let alone anything different from them?"

Because I'd helped Ingrid take out new vampires with no control. I'd kept their secrets. I'd cleaned up their messes. Every part of the arcane was a bloody, deadly mess. And I was the fucking maid.

Jay's irises bled to scarlet as he ground his teeth. "You just don't want me out there. Admit it. You've been doing this shit for years, D. Keeping me out, and I'll agree, I didn't help that." Those red eyes turned pleading as they filled with something that appeared like shame. "I was stupid and naïve and too busy keeping my head in the sand instead of backing you up—I get it. But I'm stronger now. See?"

Jay marched over to a wrought-iron candelabra, blew out the candles, and then snapped the whole fucking thing in half like a dry twig.

Jimmy buried his face in his hands to muffle his laugh as my mouth hung open in shock. And I'd thought *I* was strong.

"I'm fast, too," he added, racing toward me almost faster than I could track before stopping an inch from me. "My senses are better." He paused and then added the final nail in my argument's coffin. "I won't die on you again, D."

That had me snapping my jaw shut and returning my gaze to his maker just so I didn't start bawling. I didn't need a reminder of how I'd almost lost him. That would forever be burned in my brain just as much as losing my father was.

I'd been ready to die so Jay could live.

I'd been ready to die so he could stay human.

And I hated that a part of me was so happy he was alive that I didn't care that he'd lost his humanity. Hated that I was just that selfish.

Björn cleared his throat, trying to mask a chuckle. "Jay doesn't seem to have inherited the vampire bloodlust most fledglings have. I won't say he'll never get the urge to rend flesh, but his need to feed is admirable in the way it is controlled. I have no problem letting him back you up as long as he continues to live at the nest for the next month. After that, we'll assess where he is in his transition."

Clenching my jaw, I nodded, and pulled my phone from my back pocket. Tobin had gotten back to me about the photos, and I had a complete dossier in my inbox about Preston.

Goodie.

I had every intention of deep diving into that man's life just as soon as I could. Pulling up the first photo, I studied the sigils carved into her arms, glad they showed up in the photo plain as day. It wouldn't have been the first time magic hadn't turned up in a picture, and I no longer had a body to inspect.

Offering my phone to Hildy, I showed him the markings first. "Here. Do you recognize them?"

Hildy's eyes narrowed at the screen, his already grayed-out skin going white. "Yeah, lass. I recognize them." His shaking hand covered his mouth for a moment before he continued. "Those are the same damn markings that got me killed."

Static filled my brain for a second before I blurted, "But I thought you got killed by a poltergeist?"

Immediately, I wished I could slap myself. The only reason I knew anything about Hildy's death was from Azrael. And Azrael had told me to keep that little bit of info under my hat. *Oops*. Well, Azrael wasn't here anymore to scold me, and I needed answers.

Hildy shot me a glare before jumping to his ghostly feet. "And who told you that?"

Snorting, I rolled my eyes. "I'll give you two guesses but you're only going to need one. Who the fuck do you think told me how you died?"

Realization dawned on Hildy's face, and his eyes narrowed in indignation. "Damn Azrael to Hell and back for lyin' to ya like that. Sure, I enjoyed windin' up a ghosty or two in my time."

I scoffed. "Is that code for turning them into poltergeists for sport or…"

Hildy sent me a droll look. "*Yes*, I used 'em in battle. But I wasn't killed by one of *my* specters. No, *someone* spelled a poor soul and turned 'em into a weapon." Hildy snorted, a devilish smile curling his mouth. "Too bad they did the spell wrong, though. Left me with the power of an entire ley line, even in the afterlife."

My grin fell as his words registered.

Ley lines were created by an inordinate amount of death and destruction poised over a single place. Blood fueled them—specifically the blood of the dead. All the lines were connected and draining one could be disastrous, leaving ancestral witches without power, breaking wards that kept everything together.

Hildy had a boatload of power—power no ghost should have, grave talker or not. If he held the power of an entire ley line, and this new ghost blew up *over* a ley line, did that mean…

"Fucking shit," I muttered, shoving to my feet as my brain ran a mile a minute, putting puzzle pieces together.

In an instant, my jacket was on, and I was looking for Ingrid. I found her three rooms over in a study filled with bookshelves and heavy wood furniture, sipping on a blood bag like it was a *Capri Sun*.

"You will bring her before the council, or so help me, I'll take your head, too," she threatened, her eyes red as the blood she drank. "I don't give a shit who you made or who is loyal to you. She's fucking with the whole city, Lise."

Oh, she was doing a far sight more than that.

Ingrid's gaze found mine, and I knew my face was white as snow. "Oh, fuck. What now?"

I gestured for her to give me the phone, and reluctantly, Ingrid handed it over. Punching the "Speaker" button I let the room at large hear the sentence that had my asshole puckering and pee threatening to run down my leg.

"I'm willing to bet whoever's doing this is draining the ley lines," I began, amazed my voice didn't tremble.

"We need to find out where the other bodies were found. I'm willing to bet money they were discovered on top of a line." At the utter silence coming from the other end of the line, I continued. "She kept that under her hat, Lise. I want you to let that sink in, and then someone needs to find her before I do, you understand me?"

Lise's crisp French accent finally rattled from the receiver. "Are you threatening me, Grave Talker? That won't work out so well for you."

Snorting, I stared at the phone like it was Lise herself instead of a hunk of microchips and plastic. "Sweet Pea," I began in my deepest Southern drawl, "the sheer fact that I'm not blaming you *personally* for what your grandson has done is the only kindness you're getting from me. I'm giving you until sundown tomorrow to find Astrid by any means you deem necessary, or *I* will. And that is not a threat. That is a guarantee. You want to get your feelings hurt? Well, then, that's on you."

I didn't bother to listen to whatever Lise had to say, preferring to press the "Speaker" button again and hand it back to Ingrid. The vampire put the phone to her ear. "Darby here has been far too generous. You have less than a day. Dawn sounds about right. Fix it. Or you won't like how I choose to remedy this situation."

Ingrid pressed the "End Call" button and set her

phone down like she'd really and truly enjoy throwing it. "I'm pretty sure I hate that whole fucking family. I swear to the gods, if she doesn't come through, Mags herself will drink that bitch down."

I didn't know the family dynamics of Magdalena Dubois and her maker, but from the way she hadn't ripped Bishop's head off when he'd been snarky told me they *might* be friendly.

Or Mags didn't want blood on her clothes. Dealer's choice.

"Fabulous." A war between an ancient blood mage and the Vampire Queen of Knoxville sounded like just the thing we needed in all this mess. Pinching my brow, I said, "I'm going back to the Warden house and putting Tobin on Astrid research duty." It was better than Bishop research duty at least. With Astrid, he was more likely to actually find shit. "Then I'm going to delegate the fuck out of those sigils and see if Acker has any idea what they actually mean."

"Then you're going to heal and take a goddamn nap?" Ingrid griped, staring at me like she was disappointed at my lack of self-care. "I could travel the world with the luggage under your eyes."

Ouch.

"I love you, too," I muttered, turning to leave.

"He's fine, you know," she murmured, stopping me

in my tracks. "Jeremiah is nothing like the full-vamp fledglings. Mags already looked in on him. She said it was the same with Björn. You can trust him, babe. He isn't going anywhere."

It was a balm and a bane all at the same time. Because it didn't matter to me that Jay was a vamp or not. And it didn't matter that he was different. It mattered if his new life would alter the man I called my best friend. It mattered if this new life—the one he'd never wanted—made him a monster.

It mattered if he grew to blame me for how I'd failed him.

Without turning back to face her, I nodded.

I just hoped she was right.

6

There were only so many ways for a person like me to heal up after getting my ass kicked by a ghost bomb. Most of them involved calling ghosts to myself or visiting a cemetery. Since night had fallen in earnest by the time I'd extricated myself from Ingrid's home, I wasn't too keen on taking a jaunt through a graveyard.

But as I pulled into the drive of the Warden house, I just couldn't make myself call a single soul. Hildy was off terrorizing Acker about the sigils, and Tobin was already on finding Astrid, and Yazzie was supervising the cops processing what was left of the scene.

Jay had offered to stand watch so I could get some sleep, but since I was going to the Warden house and didn't need the backup, I told him to spend some time with Jimmy. I had a feeling I'd be calling on him soon enough, anyway.

I managed to peel myself from my car and trudge to the back entrance that led to the kitchen. The scent of coffee was high on the air, but I couldn't make myself pour a cup.

Sleep. I needed sleep.

But first, a shower. The staircase leading to my room was particularly daunting, but I hiked up those damn steps—lungs burning and legs wobbling and all. By the time I'd unloaded my weapons, got undressed, and shoved my tired bones under the spray, I was half-dead on my feet. I did the basics, cleaning the blood and soot, and who knew what else from my hair and skin, then got out.

I slipped into jammies and my softest, fuzziest robe, just barely having the wherewithal to run a brush through my hair before I hobbled out of the bathroom and to the bed.

"I leave you for five days and you've already run yourself into the ground?" a familiar silky voice growled, his presence at my back making all the hairs on my arms stand on end.

Before I told my body to move, I had my gun in my right hand and a dagger in my left. The dagger was at Aemon's throat and the gun at his gut. But there wasn't a lick of surprise on the demon's face, just censure, his crystalline-blue eyes practically glowing with heat.

He loomed over me, staring me down as his expression refused to waver, no matter what weapons I had or the compromising position he was in. "I *told you* to take care of yourself. I *told you* to rest. Why do you insist on hurting yourself, huh?"

I didn't recall him telling me anything of the sort. All I remembered was him pulling me from Jay and...

Gritting my teeth, I pressed the blade against the thick column of his throat. "I don't answer to you. Now why don't you fuck off before I give into the urge to put a bullet in your gut."

It was one thing too much. I couldn't deal with Shiloh *and* Astrid *and* ghost bombs *and* Nero *and* Bishop, on top of Aemon's fuck-shit.

No. No more.

"And here I was going to heal you all up and make it so you could actually sleep. No good deed goes unpunished, huh?"

Jay was a vampire because of him.

Jay's whole life was upside down because of him.

If he'd have just let me—

"You blame me," Aemon marveled, his eyebrows crawling up his forehead. "You—"

"Stop reading my thoughts, you dick. Those are

mine," I seethed through gritted teeth. I also may have pressed my blade just a little further into his throat.

His large hand covered mine as he pulled my knife from his flesh. "I'm not. You're just easy to figure out. A martyr down to the bone, aren't you?"

The taunt had me twisting out of his hold and shoving him back. "That's not what that was. He wasn't supposed to be there. He wasn't supposed to follow me. He shouldn't have to lose his humanity just because I'm his best friend."

Aemon rolled his eyes as he plucked the dagger from my fingers, waving it at me for a moment before he tossed it onto a side chair. "See? Martyr. 'It's my fault. I'm the bad guy. I need to suffer,'" he mocked in a high-pitched voice that was likely supposed to be mine. "Gods, why do you think he wasn't meant for exactly what happened? You can't outrun Fate, sweetheart. No one can. Not even you."

But that wasn't supposed to be Jay's path. "He—"

Aemon's fiery glare cut me off. "If it wasn't meant to be, it wouldn't have happened. You ever stop to think how much he'd hate himself if you would have died? How much this world would suffer?" His tone gentled, his expression softening. "You are important, can't you see that?"

I was and I wasn't. Sure, I had a purpose, but that

didn't mean I mattered. That I was doing any good. It was like I was the little boy with his thumb in the dam—one wrong move and everything would come crashing down on us all.

My eyes started stinging—either from tears or sheer exhaustion, I couldn't tell which, and I clenched my jaw to drive the burn away.

"I don't have time for this. Just say whatever it is you were going to say and get out." Worrying about whatever Aemon was up to was on the bottom of my list of priorities.

Then he was in my space, crowding me, despite the gun in my hand. "I was going to say that you need rest. That you haven't slept in days. That you haven't been taking care of yourself. That you need to heal." His blue eyes flashed crimson as blackness filled the room, his large body dissolving into the horned smoke monster he'd been in the caves. "Tell me, my angry little flower—are you going to start doing any of those things, or am I going to have to get creative?"

Creative? What the fuck does that mean?

Growling, I chambered a round. "What makes you think I haven't tried sleeping, huh? What makes you think that I haven't been eating? Or taking care of myself?" My shoulders hunched, the weight of everything just too much to bear. "I'm trying, okay?"

But I couldn't sleep with Bishop out there, and I *was* eating but Hildy was around all the time, and he was draining me, and I secured the property to keep all of us safe, didn't I?

And I didn't make that damn ghost blow up.

Slowly, Aemon reformed in front of me, his eyes back to the glittering blue instead of the red.

"You're trying? Well, then, that's all I can ask of you." His voice was calm, like a babbling brook or the rumble of thunder in the distance of a really good storm. You know the ones that you knew were going to give you a solid lightning show?

My eyelids drooped.

"Aww, man. You're doing that sleepy thing to me again, aren't you?" I slurred, my knees giving out. He caught me, hauling me up as sleep threatened to pull me under.

"I'll watch over you so you can sleep safe and sound. No one will get you."

Aemon didn't say the name, but we both knew what I was most afraid of—the person I saw when I closed my eyes—was Bishop. But all I could see now was darkness. My limbs felt like lead as the blackness cocooned me, letting me finally drift off into blissful sleep.

Dawn slapped me in the face the next morning, making me shy away from the sun under a pillow. The scent of coffee filled my nose, and without opening my eyes, I followed it. But it wasn't until I had planted my ass on a barstool—*my barstool*—did my lids open wide.

But I wasn't in the Warden house. I was in *my* house. My fully intact, not-burnt house. Spinning on the stool, I surveyed the living room. My favorite velvet chair in all its electric-blue glory sat in its usual spot. The windows were repaired, the walls pristine. Not a hint of smoke was in the air or soot on the walls.

I raced back to my room.

My room.

My bed.

My *things*.

Plopping to the ground, tears crawled up my throat, and because I was safe in my home, I let them out. Sobs racked from my chest as a small bit of safety settled over me. All the fear poisoning my gut, all the uncertainty and rage and just plain *dirty* feelings I couldn't get rid of poured out of me.

Aemon brought me home.

Like lancing a wound, those tears, those sobs, healed a part of me I thought had died in that cave. The part that believed in people. The part that thought humans and arcane alike were essentially good. The part that wanted more for myself than just this.

Grabbing the bedspread, I rolled into the thick

downy fabric like a burrito and let the tears take me with them, lulling myself back to sleep without the aid of a Prince of Hell.

By the time I unearthed myself from my bedspread cocoon, I was puffy, snotty, well-rested, and starving. I hadn't yet seen the man responsible for this cathartic experience, but I figured like any man, tears weren't his specialty.

The pot of coffee was still hot, though, so I poured myself a cup and sat down on my stool and sipped the blissful sweet nectar of the gods until the faint thrum of energy filled my bones.

The familiar presence at my back had me smiling into my cup.

"You know I'm here, don't you?" Aemon muttered in my ear.

Nodding, I set my cup down. "Yep. You do all this?"

He pulled out a stool and settled himself on it. "Some of it. Your friends did the rest. The magic from that witch's bomb was a doozy. I had to conjure your chair from memory. Did I get it right?"

Over my shoulder, I stared at the formerly thrifted velvet beauty and tried *not* to remember how he knew what it looked like. As far as I could recall, Aemon had only ever been inside this house while he'd been possessing me.

"It's perfect," I murmured, returning to my cup.

He hummed his agreement as he stared at his hands. "Do you think you could forgive me someday? For hurting you the way I did?"

Swallowing the lump in my throat, I tried to think about it logically. Yes, he'd possessed me. Yes, he'd killed those witches with my hands. But how could I blame him for their deaths when they were trying to kill us both? Who was to say I wouldn't have done the same? And since then, he'd been nothing but a gentleman.

He didn't have to help me sleep or heal me.

He didn't have to save me in the cave.

He didn't have to fix my house.

He didn't have to make me feel safe—and he did, damn him. After Bishop, I didn't think safe would ever be an option for me.

"Sure," I croaked, staring into my empty mug. "Don't worry about it."

We'd sat in silence for a few minutes with me wondering if my throwaway "Sure" was true and him likely doing the same when he offered me my phone.

"Here. I was going to try to keep this infernal thing from you for a few more hours, but even on silent, the damn thing is incessant."

Taking it from him, my eyes widened at the sheer

number of texts, voicemails, and missed calls—the majority from Ingrid and Jay. I set the damn thing down and plopped my head on my folded arms.

"If I tell them where I am and who I'm with, they'll never let me live it down. You know every time I'm being uppity, Ingrid threatens to summon you so I'll take a nap."

Aemon barked out a laugh, an expression of pure joy on his face as he damn near rolled off his stool. Something about his face losing a bit of its polish or maybe the complete lack of artifice, had my belly twisting and my heart speeding up.

Nope. No. Nuh-uh. No way in literal Hell.

"Oh, fuck you," I muttered as I got up to pour myself another cup of coffee.

His chuckle petered out. "How can you stand those things?"

Rolling my eyes, I took a sip of coffee as I leaned a hip against the island. "For those of us that haven't been trapped in a box for two thousand years, they are a way of life. It's better than sending a pigeon or whatever the hell ya'll did back then."

Aemon's mouth curled up on one side—a certified smirk if I ever saw one—before blackness clouded the room. A moment later he appeared at my right, no more than an inch away.

"We showed up." He waggled his brow at me before pulling a card from his suit jacket. "I don't use my phone often, but if you need me, you may call on me. Though, if you say my name out loud three times, it's just as good."

That kind gesture should not sting. It shouldn't.

But, oh, it did.

A year, sharing my body and my life with a man, and I'd never had that, and Aemon gave it freely before I ever asked. Gritting my teeth, I swallowed, allowing his words to register.

"Wait. Three times? What, like *Beetlejuice?*"

Was my throat clogged when I said that? No. No, it was not.

He frowned in confusion. "I have no idea what you're talking about."

Of course he didn't. "It's a movie. You say the spirit's name three times, and he appears wreaking havoc. It's a classic, though very problematic. Like most things from the '80s."

"Ah, I see." He reached into his jacket again and pulled out my keys. "I took the liberty of procuring your Jeep from the Warden house. Your clothes are in the closet and toiletries in the bath. Now, Blanca wouldn't give me any food—something about me being a devil from the depths of Hell—but I *did* convince her to drop a tray of tamales off in a few minutes."

Mouth agape, I stared at Aemon like he'd grown another head. "You talked to Blanca?"

The doorbell ringing cut off whatever he was going to say. Carefully, I walked to the front door, checking the peephole. Sure enough, Blanca stood on my doorstep with an aluminum tray in her hands.

Blanca was a small, curvy woman with strong, papery hands that held a ring on every finger, and a smile that was just as luminous as her spirit. I had always enjoyed being around her and her husband—even if that smile was nowhere to be seen.

As soon as I opened the door, she shoved the tray in my hands, a single eyebrow raised when she caught sight of Aemon at my back. I had never seen Blanca Bernal outside of her restaurant, and never without Martine.

"Your demon is right. You are too skinny. How come you don't come by and see me anymore, eh?" she scolded, shocking the shit out of me since she had never spoken a lick of English to me in the history of ever.

My chuckle was dark. "My life exploded, and I live in Knoxville now. It's a bit of a hike—even for food as good as yours."

A part of me wanted to ask why she'd given food to

Bishop at all. If he'd spelled her, too. But I held my tongue.

She sucked her teeth. "I heard about your papa, *mija*. I'm sorry. And we heard whispers about the mage, too."

My gaze refocused on her, allowing the comment about my dad to bounce off me instead of land. Bishop had told me that the Bernal's were *bruja*, but I didn't quite know what that meant. I knew it was Spanish for "witch," but that was about it.

"What whispers?" My gut decided at that moment to bottom out.

"That he rose the dead and murdered a bunch of wolves. That he busted open an ABI black site."

I raised my eyebrows in the affirmative. Honestly, it was better than I thought. At least everything she was saying was true.

"Anything else?" I prompted, the scent of tamales making my stomach yowl.

Her expression gentled, and I knew the worst was coming. "People are talking about the missing witches, too. They want to know if you're going to help us."

More missing witches.

Shit.

Gripping the steering wheel, I shoved the last bit of my tenth tamale in my mouth, closing my eyes briefly at the sheer bliss Blanca's cooking brought me.

It really was the little things.

"Blanca said there were three *bruja* missing from Haunted Peak. Two of her cousins and someone from her church," I barked into the speaker once I'd swallowed. I was on a conference call with Jay, Ingrid, Tobin, Shiloh, and—believe it or not—Thomas. "I need a list. An actual concrete list of who is missing, what abilities they have, who last saw them, the works. Have you found Astrid yet?"

A growl sounded down the line, one I could only assume was from Ingrid. "Yep," the small vamp said, though it was slightly muffled by the whimper of a woman. "And if she's smart, she'll tell me everything she knows before I start removing shit that won't grow back."

Aemon chuckled beside me as he unwrapped another morsel of goodness and handed it over. The tray of tamales sat between us, and he'd tried a few, claiming they were far superior to anything he'd had in the history of forever.

Yes, I shared my food.

No, I was not going to read anything into it.

I also wasn't going to tell anyone. *Ever.*

As far as the council knew, Aemon was a walking, talking menace that needed to be deported to Hell on sight. A menace I had no intention of sending back to wherever it was he came from.

And no, I wasn't going to read anything at all into that, either.

But Aemon didn't seem to be anything like the other demons I'd come across. Other than breaking out of his cage—as far as I knew—he hadn't done anything but show up to save my ass and bring me food and make me sleep.

Nope. Not thinking about that.

"Anyone pick up Preston yet? If she won't talk, we might be able to get something out of him," Shiloh offered, her new voice making my eyes twitch. I missed the smoky cadence of her true form, and the nasally tone grated on my nerves. "And who appointed Astrid Byrne to the council? That woman couldn't cast her way out of a wet paper bag."

Thomas' dark chuckle rattled down the line and all the hairs on my arms stood on end. "Oh, we picked Preston up, all right. He was crying in Ingrid's dungeon up until an hour ago. Dahlia had to put him to sleep, or else we'd be hearing his sobs right now."

There were many things I did not like about the former Vampire King of Knoxville, but as far as bounty hunting went, he was an absolute gem.

"Fabulous. I'll be there in twenty minutes. Try not to kill him before I can question the asshole, would you?"

"I make no promises," Thomas replied, irritating as ever. "The bastard bit me when shooting me didn't work. He's lucky I didn't drain him dry and string him up by his toenails."

Honestly? That was fair. If some douche canoe shot me, I'd probably do the same.

"Fair enough. I'll be there soon."

Then I clicked off and shoved another tamale into my face. The corn and stewed pork and the magical spices burst in a cornucopia of flavors across my tongue, and I had to force my eyeballs not to roll up into my head while driving. Interstate 75 was a bitch on most days, but today it was a wrecked ruin.

Almost like someone was purposely trying to keep me from Knoxville by any means necessary.

Narrowing my eyes on the jumble of cars in front of me, I chewed the blissful morsel. "This isn't you, right? You aren't making the citizens of Tennessee play bumper cars for fun, are you?"

Aemon's shoulders stiffened in my peripheral vision, and I couldn't help rolling my eyes. A part of me wondered why he was still here. In the past, he'd just up and disappeared once I was healed or properly chastised or whatever.

"Aemon?" I growled, my hands tightening on the steering wheel. It was one thing to kidnap me so I could sleep and give me food. It was quite another to actively keep me from my job.

Slumping in his seat, he waved his hand at the windshield. "Fine." He petulantly crossed his arms over his chest. "I wanted you to finish your food. What's that phrase humans use? Oh, right. *So sue me.*"

Pressing my lips together so I wouldn't laugh, I focused on the traffic that now seemed to be flowing nicely once again. I did not like how good that felt, nor did I appreciate the butterflies setting up shop in my belly. I should not be fawning all over his kindness, or want to embrace the sweetness of him...

No. No way. Not again. Not ever again.

I wasn't doing that bullshit softening thing for another man, no matter who or what he was. Accepting help, wanting affection, wanting a partner—none of those things ever worked out for me. And the first time I even had an inkling of any of it, the first time I opened up at all, he turned out to be a monster.

"Why are you doing this? What do you get out of helping me?" I asked, frowning at the road ahead. It was a question I should have asked Bishop but didn't. I just walked in there blind and let him set up shop in my heart. A heart he molded to his will. "Is it guilt you feel? Like you owe me?"

Because why else would he be here? Why else would he watch me like that? He needed something or he felt guilty. There wasn't an option three.

"For a smart woman, you sure are dense sometimes," he muttered, but there didn't seem to be any heat in his words.

Just resolve.

Somehow, I figured that was worse.

"You didn't save any for me?" Jay whined when he noticed my empty tray of Blanca's tamales. There weren't even any crumbs of masa left, just the corn husks and my full belly. I was content and well-fed for probably the first time in a while, my eyes no longer droopy, and my bones no longer creaking.

And I refused to think about how I got that way, wishing I could just erase the demon from my brain. Aemon had disappeared not long after my probing questions, unwrapping the last tamale and handing it over. He told me to take care of myself, and then he was gone. A part of me missed him just a little bit.

Granted, it was a part I fully planned on shoving so far down in my emotional well that I'd never see it again, but it was there all the same.

Swallowing hard, I shot Jay a shit-eating grin. It was fake—just like so many of my smiles were these days— but I did it. "When have you ever been able to trust me around food?"

Jay speared me with a glare. "Never. Even when we were kids, you'd steal all the yummies, you hag. I'm a growing boy, too, you know."

Slipping my arm around his waist, I gave him the mother of all squeezes. "But you still love me, though, right?"

He squeezed me back, his new strength nearly cracking my ribs. "I guess. If you want to get technical."

"They kill anybody in there?" I asked, pulling away to grab my duffle from the back hatch of my Jeep. As much as I loved my house, as much as I appreciated what Aemon had done for me, I couldn't stay in Haunted Peak.

But my house being restored meant that I could have a home there if I wanted. It meant there was a place to go if I needed a break. A place that was just mine and no one else's.

"Not yet, but if Astrid doesn't start talking, bloodshed is not off the menu," he replied, looking me over with a critical eye. "I'm glad you got some rest and some food. I'm glad you took a break."

I didn't want to tell him my break was not of my own volition, so I simply nodded instead. I'd had every intention of sleeping when I'd gotten to the Warden house. Whether or not that was actually in the cards was another story altogether. Aemon just sped that process along.

"Why do you smell like smoke, though?"

Raising my eyebrows, I shrugged innocently and beat feet for Ingrid's office. "No idea."

I'd almost made it to the back door before an incredibly strong hand stopped me, nearly pulling me off my feet and smacking my duffle against my legs. "Your rested, healed, and satisfied appearance wouldn't have anything to do with a very handsome Prince of Hell, would it?"

Shaking my head, I studiously avoided Jay's eyes. "Nope. Nothing at all."

Jay let me go and took a giant step back. "You *liar*. From what Jimmy and Ingrid told me, the man is finer than a cashmere sweater at fifty percent off, but—"

Clenching my teeth, I swiveled on a heel and marched through the back door of Ingrid's house. "But nothing. I don't know what you're talking about."

Yes, I was lying my ass off.

Yes, I was purposely avoiding the warm squishy feelings I got when I thought about my restored chair.

Yes, I might have had a teensy, tiny almost imperceptible appreciation for Aemon's drop-dead gorgeous, good looks.

But I had enough emotional damage to fill the Grand Canyon and bigger fish to fry. Missing witches. People dying. Ley lines draining. Ghosts exploding.

Big. Fish.

I dropped my duffle next to the stairs and weaved around Thomas and Jimmy to get into the office. The scent of burning flesh was high on the air as I spied a very put-out Astrid tied to a chair with what *appeared* to be magical ropes?

Next to her loomed an irritated Bastian who was

flexing his hand like it hurt. Shock had my steps stuttering. Sebastian Cartwright was my sister's boyfriend and said sister was nowhere to be found. Trust me, I'd looked.

"What are you doing here?" I blurted, offering the big man a hug.

Bastian gave me a slight smile, accepting me in a one-armed embrace. His other hand was too busy keeping Astrid in check. "Hello to you, too. Sloane is otherwise indisposed, so she sent me. Seems like you have a witch problem."

My gaze fell to the witch bitch in question, her electric ropes searing her skin every time she struggled against them.

Bastian had never been a fount of information, but it was concerning that Sloane hadn't come at all. "She okay?"

Normally, I wouldn't bother to ask, but the sheer fact that Azrael had died made my insides twist every time I thought of her in danger. Death came for us all in the end, right?

Bastian's smile was forced this time, which did nothing for my level of concern. "Fine. Nothing for you to worry about."

I wanted to tell him just how bad of a liar he was, but I was interrupted by the source of my issues herself.

"Excuse me," Astrid barked—a mighty show, considering she was bound to a chair, "but I thought you were here to talk to *me*."

A woman tutted from the couch to my left, and it took my brain a second to recognize that Lise Fucking Dubois was inspecting her nails with an irritated expression on her face.

Yes, well, join the club.

"Gods above, Astrid. Do you not know when to shut the fuck up?"

I'd been so focused on Bastian's sudden appearance that I'd missed the council head completely.

"At least I'm not sitting idly by while they torture someone right in front of me," Astrid jeered, her mouth twisted into a scowl.

Three witches had died so far and countless were missing, and she wanted to keep the information to herself?

No.

Not just no, but *fuck* no.

"Oh, you think this is torture?" I asked, gesturing to the ropes. "Okay."

A moment later my hand glowed gold, and I shoved my power down onto the woman. The magical ropes flickered out as the pressure landed on her shoulders.

The chair collapsed beneath her as I increased the weight.

Astrid clawed at her throat, the air refusing to get to her lungs.

At the count of five, I called the golden light back to me as I knelt by her head, my gun tucked under her chin. "Miss ma'am, I can do that all. Fucking. Day. I can make you pray for death. And when she comes—*and she will*—I will let her rip your soul to shreds while I fucking watch."

Astrid's eyes widened as her pale face bloomed with color, but her mouth snapped shut when she caught sight of my glowing palm. No more bitchy antics. No more stalling. I'd just as soon put a bullet in her brain and take her soul than deal with this bullshit.

"Now, I can get what I want to know from your very soul or your lips. Either way, I'm going to get the information I need." My smile was pure evil as I surveyed the redheaded terror. "You pick."

"Dear sweet mother of the Fates. I thought Sloane was frightening," Thomas muttered, plopping on the couch after he flicked Lise's feet off a cushion. "I don't know if I'm turned on or scared shitless."

I flipped Thomas off while still holding the gun under Astrid's chin. "I'm not hearing any information, Astrid. Talk."

Astrid narrowed her eyes at me. "You can't do this. I'm a council memb—"

"Sweetie," I barked, pointing to Lise, "if her grandson walked into this room, I'd put a bullet in his head *in front* of her. She's sitting right there watching me. No one cares who you *think* you are. You need to start thinking about what life you have left before I damn well take it from you. Information. *Now*."

Her jaw clenched as her face got redder, her internal debate slow as fucking molasses. "Fine. But you can't go off half-cocked."

Me? Go off willy-nilly? Never.

"Someone is doing death magic to drain the ley lines," she said, like it was some huge revelation.

Pinching my brow, I tried to stave off the headache this absolute dumpster fire of a person was causing. "I know that already."

"Well, do you know that the ones that turn up dead *aren't* the ones that have gone missing?"

Dropping my hand, I stared at the witch.

"That, I didn't know."

8

Astrid had her ass planted in one of the three null rooms in Ingrid's basement. Why Ingrid had a dungeon full of null rooms was anyone's guess, but I was sure as hell glad she had them to suppress the witch bitch's power. There was only so much I could do without the help of the ABI—an agency I wanted nowhere near Astrid for the time being.

While they had cells, a prison, and manpower, they also unfortunately had more corruption than a human politician, more infiltrators than I knew what to do with, and a prison system I never wanted to see the inside of again.

Plus, no one—and I did mean no one—at the ABI would even speak to me right now. After the Bishop bullshit, the Davenport execution, the Essex escape, and the threat of the council dissolving the ABI in Knoxville? I was *persona non grata* for the foreseeable future. Hell, I was lucky they hadn't recalled Yazzie, Tobin, or Acker yet, otherwise I'd be screwed trying to do this damn job by myself.

In the cell beside Astrid—also a null—was Preston, passed out cold. Ingrid informed me that once she hadn't been able to trance the poor cop, she'd stuck him in there to cool his heels. I couldn't blame her one bit. The absolute last thing we all needed was a sleeper arcaner getting the drop on us in the middle of this bullshit.

Our cup was full.

"You know it has to be Nero," Astrid murmured, her pitying gaze on Ingrid. "Just look at what he did in Crete."

I had no idea what Nero had done in Crete, however, the sheer body count from that vampire was in the hundreds of thousands—if not millions—and from the files Tobin had accumulated, his depravity knew no bounds. A part of me thought it was funny that Astrid was in a cell, and she had the gall to pity Ingrid. Though, considering who Ingrid's sire was, well, it sort of made sense.

If I had to live for the rest of forever with that man as my maker? *Yikes.*

"And how do we know it's not you doing this?" I asked, not really believing Astrid was smart enough or evil enough to put this bullshit together. "You clearly have a grudge against me and the members of the council who support me. You know exactly what I can do, and how I do it. And what was your area of specialty, again?" I tapped on my lip, pretending to think.

Witches usually chose an area where their abilities flourished. Some were fabulous in the garden—others could whip up a potion like it was nothing. There were witches who loved curses and hexes, ones that worked with fire, and some had an affinity for the dead.

"You broke up an entire coven," she seethed through gritted teeth. "Of course I hate you. I think you should burn for what you did."

Rolling my eyes, I settled onto my chair. Witches and their burning. Jesus. "Sure. And what would you have done if you were in my shoes? Let them go? Let them continue to practice? Let them try again? It was disband them, or kill them all. I chose the least murder-y option."

Because it was a very near thing for me to not just kill them all. I wondered if she knew how close I'd come to that very end for those witches.

"How do you know they would ha—"

"Their minds were made up," I barked, cutting her

off. "And they hadn't been spelled or lied to or coerced. They knew exactly what they were doing and who they were backing up. They knew, Astrid. Funny. You never scold me about the ghoul nest I disbanded on the same day. Biased much?"

If Astrid had any power in that cell, she would have cut me in half with her mind. "Ghouls are violent creatures. Why would I care about their disbandment?"

"And yet, they were just hired muscle. Not the masterminds."

No, the mastermind had been my mother wearing Shiloh's face. And every time I thought about Mariana, the more I thought about my dad. Chest aching, I tried not to let that pain show.

Astrid stood, knocking the chair in her cell to the ground. "I'm not the bad guy here. All I did was tell Preston to call me if anything weird showed up on his side of town. How is that a bad thing?"

"For fuck's sake," Ingrid muttered, pinching her brow like she was trying to keep her brain from exploding. "First of all, he's a human cop."

Well, that was still up for debate, considering Ingrid couldn't trance him, but whatever.

"Second, you didn't tell anyone about the murders," she continued, counting them off on her fingers. "Third, you refused to talk to us about said murders, even after a fucking ghost exploded. Fourth, you knew about witch abductions but said absolutely nothing about it to anyone. Honestly, do you need me to spell it out in crayon or something? This is the most overt case of shady shit you have come up with yet, and I'm not even done. Like, are you being purposefully obtuse, or are you just that dumb?"

Astrid's face went beet-red, and she even had the gumption to pick up her chair and throw it at the cell bars. "Fuck you, Ingrid. You know if she knew about this shit from the jump, she'd just get in the way," she said pointing at me. "How was I supposed to keep Nero from finding out I was on to him, huh?"

Jesus in a fucking manger, she was an idiot. We had no proof Nero was even in town. We had nothing but whispers, which amounted to him as a boogeyman in children's stories. We were missing a big thread, and Astrid's circle-jerk of a confession was doing my head in. I had half a mind to yank her out of that cell by her hair and waterboard her until she gave up every single detail.

"Darby?" Jay called, and I gladly took my leave, though with the tone he was using, I had no hope whatever it was he was going to tell me would be any better than the shitshow I was leaving.

Trekking up the basement steps, I met my best

friend's gaze and knew it was no good, very bad news. "What now?"

"There's another one. Morningside Park."

Another dead witch in another human space.

Fucking perfect.

I had half a mind to bring riot gear and a helmet with me as I stepped onto the circular walk that surrounded Morningside Park. Another freaking circle. This time, though, I had an inkling of what I was walking into, and luckily, there were no human cops on the scene.

The next time I saw him, I'd be kissing Tobin right on the mouth. Well, not really. He'd probably disintegrate on the spot and then I'd be down an agent. He'd managed to rig a plug-in that monitored all calls into the Knoxville PD, the Tennessee State Troopers, and any 911 calls requesting an ambulance for presumed dead women and rerouted all the weird ones to us.

Seriously. Could kiss him.

A part of me wished the arcane was out in the open. That we didn't have to hide our shit from humans. But I didn't see how the transition from "Only humans exist" to "There are monsters among you" would work out. The torches and pitch forks would get unearthed posthaste.

"This is a mess, huh?" Jay muttered—the joy of my partner being back tempered by the twist in my gut.

Was it so wrong that I wanted him in Bubble Wrap and a helmet? My face must have said as much because he gave me a withering glare.

"I'm fine. Not burning in the sun or starving for blood or anything. See?" He revealed his blunted teeth and blinked his blue eyes. "You don't need to worry about me."

Giving him a little hip check, I rolled my eyes. "I didn't say anything. Leave me and my unvoiced PTSD freak-out alone. I had to hold your bloody throat together with my bare hands. I'm allowed a little time to adjust."

Groaning, he pulled his pocketknife from his belt. "Watch," he ordered before slicing the blade against his skin. Jay had kept that blade as sharp as a razor since his mama had given it to him when he turned twelve.

Gasping, I reached for the wound, only to realize it was already healed by the time I got to it.

Unbidden by the healing, I took my messenger bag and started beating him with it. "Jesus fucking Christ, Jeremiah." *Smack.* "I just told you." *Smack.* "That I held your neck together." *Smack.* "With my bare." *Smack.* "Fucking." *Smack.* "Hands." *Smack.* "And you do that bullshit? I ought to kick you in the balls, you fucking idiot."

"I'm sorry," Jay grumbled, holding his hands up in surrender—one still bloody, if healed, and the other one perfectly clean. "I thought it would be a good demonstration. No need to get your feathers ruffled."

Darkness settled over us both like a blanket before it quickly lifted. An extremely angry Aemon stood in between my best friend in the world and myself, his back to me. He loomed over Jay, his body bigger, wider, meaner than I'd ever seen it—his form solid, even if his blazing eyes and fiery horns were on full display.

It should have surprised me that he was here. It should have made me screech at the lack of privacy since he had to have been watching me somehow, but I just couldn't make myself. Not when I heard what was coming out of his mouth.

"You apologize, and you make it sincere, and you do it right now," Aemon growled, his hand gently holding me away as I tried to get in between them. "She damn near gave her life up so you could stay human, and if I hadn't ripped her off you, she'd be dead right now."

That had me freezing, but Jay stumbled back a step, like this was new information. Maybe he didn't remember everything that happened in the caves, maybe he didn't know it was happening, but I would have figured Jimmy would have told him.

"You *do not* play about it, or get your feelings hurt, or anything else but be eternally fucking grateful that this woman loves you to the end of the universe and back. That she'd give up every ounce of happiness and her future to see you breathing. You'd better not think another thought about anything other than how lucky you are to have her until the end of your undoubtedly long life. Understand?"

Jay stopped looking at Aemon and focused on me in all his fanged-out, red-eyed glory. "What's he talking about, D?"

"Nothing," I gritted out, glaring at Aemon. Didn't we have bigger things to worry about than this? Did it really matter that no one had told Jay what I'd done?

"You *turd*," he gasped. "Tell me he's lying."

Raising my eyebrows at Aemon, I gestured to Jay. "See? He didn't know. Calm down, tiger."

Aemon's glowing red gaze faded to blue as he narrowed his eyes on me. I had a feeling my dismissal was about to go over like a lead balloon.

"Jay, meet Aemon. Aemon, this is my best friend, Jay."

Jay narrowed his eyes, inspecting the Prince of Hell like he was a side of beef or a particularly pricey jacket.

"You'll understand if I reserve judgment until you prove yourself?"

Aemon's smile was pure challenge. "And you'll understand that she won't be sacrificing herself for anyone ever again. Got it?"

Jay's eyebrows rose and then his gaze fell on the necklace at my throat before returning to the demon in front of him. That necklace had broken the hold Bishop had over me. It kept me safe from any and all magical attacks.

Then I remembered the zombies.

So maybe not *all* magical attacks.

"Okay, you can stick around. For now. But I'll be watching you." Jay pointed two fingers at his eyes and then directed them at Aemon. "Don't think I can't put you right back in that box where she found you."

Aemon's mouth quirked into a grin. "I'd expect nothing less from Darby's family."

Jay nodded and moved toward Jimmy and Yazzie, who were both standing on the sidewalk, mouths agape.

"You do realize you still have horns, right?" I muttered out of the side of my mouth.

A single blink later, and Aemon's horns were gone, almost like they'd been a figment of my imagination.

"Snoop much?" I muttered, gently slapping him in

the gut with the back of my hand. "What are you doing here?"

Crossing his arms, Aemon raised a single blond eyebrow at me. "The last time I left you alone, you nearly got gnawed on by zombie wolves. The time before that, you got attacked by real-live wolves. Don't get me started on the exploding ghost. If I hadn't yanked you out of there, you'd be a crispy critter by now."

Fair enough. I'd wondered who'd pulled me out of there when that ghost went Chernobyl on me. To find out it was Aemon did a number on my stomach, the fact he'd been looking out for me this whole time softening me just a bit.

"You, my angry little flower, are a full-time job." He gestured to the circular walk taped off with a police line. "Plus, this mess has Nero's stink all over it. Two birds, one stone, and all that."

That had me standing straighter. "You mean you can smell him?"

Aemon stared at the grassy knoll with the body in the middle of it. "Figure of speech. I mean that this isn't the first time he's done something like this."

A two-thousand-year-old vampire had done a ley line power grab more than once? What were the chances? "What do you mean by that?"

"Do you think selling his soul was the first thing he tried?"

Snorting, I moved toward the body as I pulled gloves from my bag. "Ya think that might have been a clue to maybe *not* make a deal with the crazy man bent on power? I'm not telling you how to do your job or anything, but what exactly is the criteria for a soul-selling transaction?"

Aemon's smile widened, a devilish gleam in his eyes. "Let's hope you never have to find out."

9

By the time I'd crossed the tape, Aemon had once again disappeared, his presence making everyone else uneasy. Yazzie shot me a "What the fuck" wide-eyed expression as he helped Shiloh finish her salt circle.

Shrugging, I focused on the body instead. It wasn't like I could answer anyone about Aemon and whatever was going on between us. Not that anything *was* going on.

Nope.

Dead body.

There was an actual dead body in front of me that needed my attention. I most definitely should not be worrying about the sinfully hot man who took care of me and restored my favorite chair from memory.

But hadn't I done this song and dance before? Someone showed me the slightest bit of affection and appreciation, and there I was falling all over them like a love-sick teenager on crack. How was this Aemon situation any different than how I'd been suckered by Bishop? All Bishop had to do was bring me food, and I'd been half in love with him.

That's different. He was spelling you. It wasn't your fault.

I'd told that to survivors, too. And I believed it. For *them*.

I was supposed to know better.

I was supposed to see the signs.

I was supposed to—

"Darby," Jay murmured, laying a hand on my shoulder, "are you okay?"

His touch made me flinch, and I had to force myself to not run for the fucking hills or something. Hell, it took everything in me not to reach for my gun.

"Yeah," I croaked, wiping my nose with the back of my hand. "I'm great."

Yes, I was tearing up.

Yes, I needed a truckload of therapy and a vacation.

Yes, I was lying to my best friend.

Whatever.

I handled everything so much better when I was mad —when I wasn't dwelling and just knocking the shit out of someone. But there wasn't anyone for me to hit, just a dead body that needed my attention, and hopefully no exploding ghosts.

"There," Shiloh called. "The circle is done. Whatever is live inside can't do any harm outside of the ward."

Given that the last time I'd gone to a body, the ghost had gone nuclear, setting a ward seemed like the only option for keeping everyone safe. Searching the scene for the tell-tale wisp of gray, I was disheartened to find the park empty. A part of me was glad. The lack of ghosts and graves and cracked pavement meant this murder might not be related to the death at the National Cemetery.

Then again, coincidences just weren't a regular happenstance in my life.

Gloves and booties on, I minced over the ward and through the tufts of grass toward the woman draped in a sheet. Dark curls matted with blood spilled from the top, and large pools stained the drape crimson. By the time she'd been killed, and we'd gotten the word, this woman couldn't have been dead long.

Normally, Morningside Park was filled with people, but today this particular part of the park was a ghost town—no pun intended. I didn't have high confidence that we'd glean any witnesses from the area.

The park had many sections, including the forest-laden disc golf area we were currently in. About a football field away, a playground and gazebo were situated near a quaint clubhouse and meeting areas. The screeches of laughing children at the playground sounded through the trees, as if any moment an impressionable child could walk through them and witness this horrendous scene.

Just the thought of what occurred at the National Cemetery happening here made me want to vomit. What if our protections failed? What if the explosion was bigger than before? What if just by intervening, we sentenced these people to death?

"Can we clear the park?" I asked, not looking up from the blood-soaked drape.

The shuttering *click* of Jimmy's camera taking a picture sounded nearby. "Not without drawing unwanted attention to ourselves. I've made it so no one wants to come back here, though."

I supposed that would just have to do.

Gently, I pulled the drape back. I'd done this hundreds of times in my years as a homicide detective, and each time, it hurt my heart. This was someone's kid, someone's sibling. Somebody, somewhere loved this person, cared that they were gone.

I figured it was the reason I appreciated the ghosts I could see—even if it made me half-crazy sometimes. It was a chance to help someone. A chance to catch a bad guy. And—if I was being truly honest—my competitive ass loved to have all the inside information.

The woman was a bloody mess, her throat half-gone, but her face didn't carry the fear one would expect from such a wound. Even in death and the muscles losing their strength, faces tended to still carry the terror on them. No, her expression was nothing short of blissful. As if she'd been tranced or something.

Trancing to me immediately pointed to the blood-drinking variety of the arcane. But none of the Dubois vampires had to trance their prey. They had plenty of willing donors and blood bags besides.

Carefully, I lifted her chin. The wounds were small, like she'd been killed by a small fox or a midsized dog or something. Did foxes even kill people? Should I be on the lookout for a particularly jumpy cocker spaniel?

But no one would just sit there while a rabid dog gnawed on their throat. "Jay, can you hand me a ruler?"

He dug inside my messenger bag for the pocket ruler I kept, passing it over. "It smells like vampire, but—"

I picked up exactly where his thoughts were going. "The bites are too small. It's almost like a—"

"Child bit her," Jay finished for me, the unease in his voice matching the dip in my gut.

We only knew of one child vampire, and there was no way she'd do a thing like this. "It wasn't her."

He rolled his eyes at me. "Of course it wasn't. But it was someone her size. It was someone with her general build and strength and abilities. Look at the fraying of the flesh. Someone gnawed on her, D. They glutted themselves on all they could get, and they *chewed* on her throat to get whatever was left. That doesn't tell me good things about their mental state—vampire or not."

"So, on top of a possible ancient vamp with major *ick* vibes, someone draining witches and ley lines, we also have a half-rabid child vamp on the loose? Is that what you're saying?"

Even though I'd asked the question, I already knew the answer. And that particular rundown of all the shit going on didn't even take into account the death mage on the loose or the ABI imploding in on itself or the prisoners missing from the black site Essex had been liberated from.

Why was Knoxville so fucking complicated?

Jay shot me a leveling glance over the body. "And I'm willing to bet all three of those things are related, because you know what I say about coincidences, don't you?"

Grumbling, I said, "That they don't and have never existed, and anyone who says otherwise is trying to avoid jail time. Yeah, yeah. I heard you the first gazillion times you said it."

"Wait a minute," Shiloh breathed, the alarm in her voice making me stand on creaking knees to scan the area for threats. She leaned closer to the body, squinting her eyes. "Jimmy, can you get a close-up on her face?"

Jimmy did as asked—his expression just as confused as all of ours likely were. He passed the camera to Shiloh, and her new face paled at the picture on the display.

"Don't leave us hanging, Shi," I barked, my gut twisting hard.

"That's Candace Moore. She was a Knoxville Coven witch until she got kicked out for stealing from her fellow coven members. I remember it was all anyone could talk about for weeks when I was a kid—how she betrayed them. A week after she was cast out, it was discovered that it wasn't her that stole at all. It was a hiding jinx that went awry."

It was good that we had a name to go with the body, but that still didn't tell us what happened to her or explain Shiloh's reaction. At my blank stare, she dropped the hammer.

"Candace Moore killed herself. Twenty years ago."

Not only did that give me pause, but it had me

backing away from the body like it might actually explode.

"No offense, but I'd be willing to bet the liver temp would beg to differ," Jay said from his crouch by the body. "Are you sure it's her?"

"Positive. Candace used to babysit me when Mom was too busy. I'd know her anywhere."

I pulled off a glove and yanked my phone from my back pocket, scrolling to the crime scene pictures before the ghost bomb. "What about her? Do you know this woman?"

Shiloh scanned the photos, her new face screwing up in chagrin. "No, but Astrid has to. She signs off on all new coven members. Does Ingrid have a copy of this?"

Attaching the photos to a text, I sent them off to Ingrid, along with a little message to badger Astrid into looking at them. "She does now."

"Good. I'm going back," Shiloh said, handing my cell over to me. "Astrid has to know both of these women and that means at the very least they will get put to rest by their families."

And hopefully Ingrid hasn't killed her already in the midst of her interrogation.

I nodded, stuffing my phone back in my pocket, finding Acker who was studiously *not* looking at the body. I'd had a hunch he'd been avoiding the last one.

"Take Acker with you. We'll be wrapping things up here soon."

Ambrose seemed grateful, his shoulders losing a bit of tension as he skirted around the circle. "Thanks, boss. You want me to call Tobin and get all the info we can on Candace Moore?"

Giving Acker shit about not wanting to be around blood and death would be poor form. Being a Mormo, he likely desired blood just as much as any vamp would—even if he had his powers bound.

"Sure do," I murmured, slapping him on the shoulder before stepping close. "Next time, just tell me you don't want to come to these, okay? Not everyone can do this part, and that's cool with me. But study the files. Whoever did this needed blood for that bomb. See if the sigils mean anything to you."

His smile appeared like pure relief. "Already on it. So far, I've put them to an ancient form of Latin, but I'll need to dig more to get the exact dialect. Hildy's been helping."

"Fabulous." Sweet Mary in a manger, if my grandfather was "helping," I had to wonder if Acker was ever going to get any rest until this particular puzzle was solved.

Shiloh and Acker took off, and Jay and I went back to the body, cataloguing her injuries while Jimmy took as many pictures as he could. It sucked that there was no specter attached to this body, no way to find out exactly what happened, or who hurt her.

I said as much to Jay, his brow furrowing in the way it always did when he did *not* like the words coming out of my mouth. "That's the second body in two days that hasn't had a ghost attached to it. How often would you say that happens?"

Huffing out a dispirited chuckle, I shook my head. "Almost never. Sure, some souls move on immediately, but people who have been murdered generally stick around to see their killer caught. There have been a few that go quickly—staying just long enough to give me one last message, and the car wrecks and gentle deaths go quick. But murders?"

I gave him a look that said everything I needed to say. Spirits of the murdered dead were tenacious, hounding me day and night until their killers were found. My first year on the force nearly did me in, and my first year as a detective? If Hildy hadn't shown me how to keep them out of my house, I would have never gotten any sleep.

"At least there doesn't seem to be any active spells," Jimmy offered, getting one last picture before stowing his camera. "I can't see any magic here at all, just a residue of a spent spell. Whatever happened here, it's over already."

With nothing left to do, I had Tobin call in the human authorities. This woman's body needed to be processed, even if they would likely never find the killer. A part of me wished I could trust the ABI, that I could trust them to not cover this mess up or use it for their own gain. That I could believe in a single person...

But I did know a single, solitary person in the ABI—save for Yazzie, Acker, and Tobin, that I could trust. Reaching for my phone again, I dialed a number I didn't have to use very often. Three rings later, Sarina's voicemail kicked on. I hadn't seen her since I left Ingrid's to go back to work.

At the beep, I hung up, preferring to text her instead. Most days I'd rather toss my phone into a running blender than leave a voicemail. Plus, most voicemails were just a plea to call me back.

A text would suffice.

I have questions about a case. Can you call me back when you get a chance?

Ugh. It sounded so formal, but Sarina and I were in a weird place right now.

We gathered everything that pointed to anyone ever being here and loaded up, the drape and gloves in biohazard bags that would need to be tossed in an incinerator soon.

Just as I was about to close the hatch, Aemon

appeared at my side, nearly making me come out of my skin. Dagger in hand, it was at his gut before I realized it was even him. Granted, he also had a gun at his temple from Jay, and a sword at his throat from Jimmy, so I hadn't been the only one to overreact.

"Jesus, fuck, Aemon," I gasped. "You're worse than Hildy with that shit."

Aemon's smile was practically jovial as he held up his hands. "So noted. Care to call your friends off? Hurting them is not on the agenda."

Rolling my eyes, I waved them off. "It's fine, guys."

Slowly, each man stowed their weapons, but Jay pointed at his own eyes again before directing them at the Prince of Hell.

"You need a bell or something," I muttered, sheathing my dagger.

"No," he countered, "what I need is for you to go straight to Ingrid's with no detours. I have an errand to run, and I can't watch you."

Well, didn't that just grate on every nerve I had.

Squinting at the demon, I put my hands on my hips. "First of all, you don't tell me what to do. Second, what am I, a houseplant? I am not your responsibility, your charge, or your girl. I don't need you to *watch* me. I have survived nearly thirty years on this planet without you, I'll be just fine on my own."

Pursing his lips, Aemon narrowed his eyes. "I see." They began glowing scarlet as his form grew larger, his horns making another appearance.

"How about this," he growled, his face mere inches from mine, "if anything happens to you while I'm gone —helping *your* sister, in case you were curious—I'll hold each and every man in that vehicle with you responsible."

First Bastian topside, and now Aemon going to help? What the fuck was going on with my sister?

"Why would you be helping Sloane?" I asked, my heart pumping double-time. I wasn't scared of Aemon— not that I could pinpoint exactly *why* I wasn't, but whatever. I was worried about the death deity that had failed to arrive when a ghost blew up. A ghost that couldn't be absorbed, talked to, or well, *anything*.

Aemon shook his head. "I'm not allowed to say. I was given very strict instructions to keep my trap shut. And your sister is vicious. I'm not getting on the wrong side of her. I like my life *outside* of a box, thank you."

"Vicious is a family trait, so why don't you keep your threats to yourself?" I warned, skirting around the demon and opening the driver's side door. "You'll lay a finger on my guys over my dead body."

Aemon's fiery gaze narrowed into slits. "Then you'd better be sure no one lays a finger on that very alive body until I'm back." He ducked his currently huge body so he could look Yazzie—who was sitting shotgun— right in the eye. "Am I understood?"

"Fuck off, Aemon," I growled. "Go help my sister do whatever mysterious task you can't tell me about and quit threatening people."

In an instant, his red eyes, horns, and huge features were gone. "As you wish. Stay safe, my angry little flower."

"Get fucked," I said as I slid into the seat.

His smile went wide. "That could be arranged, you know."

Flipping him off, I punched the ignition button and slammed my door. As soon as my seatbelt was buckled, I threw the Jeep in "Drive" and hauled ass away from the damn demon with the too-perfect smile and adorably protective nature that made my belly go funny.

I was not falling for that shit again. Never. Again.

I could practically feel Jay's mouth open from the back seat. "Not a word, Jeremiah. Not. One. Word."

"I didn't say anything," Jay grumbled, pouting.

"You were gonna." And he was, too. He was turning red from how hard he was holding in his questions.

Switching on the radio, I let the rock music blast through the speakers as I headed back to Ingrid's. I had half a mind to stop literally anywhere just out of spite, but there was nowhere else I needed to be. At the turnoff to Beacon Hills, I enjoyed the forest-lined quiet road and the absolute silence from the three men in the cab.

Okay, so my hands *might* have been glowing to keep that train going, but whatever.

A train that quickly ended with a shout from the back. I barely had time to slam on my brakes when a man larger than any I'd ever seen stepped out into the middle of the road.

Right before my Jeep slammed into him, he rammed both fists into the hood, his evil smile gleeful as the force of his blow sent us skyward.

Aemon was gonna be *pissed*.

10

Of all the things to think of, it was the sheer lack of car accidents I'd had in my life. In my nearly fifteen years of driving, I hadn't once gotten a speeding ticket or crumpled the fender of my car. I'd been studious in Driver's Ed, getting nearly a perfect score on my test.

Well, I'd officially broken my car accident cherry, and man, it was a doozy.

Glass was everywhere, the Jeep was upside down, and everything hurt. The bite of the seatbelt digging into my shoulder and middle was only slightly tempered by the absolute railroad spike of an ache in my skull, and that said nothing about the blood running into my hair from a cut somewhere on my head.

It took a second to remember that I'd hit someone—

or rather that someone had hit me—and even longer to remember I hadn't been alone in the Jeep. Everything was so quiet, the only sound the faint ticking of the demolished engine trying to cool down and the hiss of my radiator leaking. In the back of my mind, I was crying for my beautiful car, but the front part—that was mostly addled, and half-crazed with adrenaline—had some sense.

Kind of.

"Someone talk to me," I groaned, trying to turn my head before my neck made a violent protest. I didn't know how many times we'd rolled over, but it had to have been a lot.

Faintly, the sound of the fight outside the Jeep filtered into my brain—punches and shouts and the scuffle of shuffling feet. Sluggishly, I tried unbuckling my seatbelt, but with fumbling fingers and the counterweight of well, *me*, the only way out was to cut the belt.

Dad used to tell me to keep a hook knife in my car for just such a problem, and I'd always thought it was a good idea. Too bad the damn thing was in the glove compartment and out of reach.

A hand stretched into my broken window, and for a split second, I was grateful. For the single moment, I thought I was getting help. Then my brain finally registered the sheer size of the hand and the cruel, twisted face that followed it.

"Aww, wassamatter, Warden, you stuck?" the man jeered, latching onto my seatbelt and giving it a tug. It was the same fucker who'd slammed his fist into the hood of my Jeep.

The belt gave way, and that absolute catcher's mitt of a hand grabbed onto the front of my shirt and dragged me from the wreck. Up close and personal with the guy, I had to peg him as a ghoul—the sheer size and strength a dead giveaway.

Dead giveaway.

Snorting, I let out a little chuckle, which earned me a spiteful scowl.

"Oh, you think this is funny, do you?" He tightened his hold on my shirt, nearly choking me. "Come on, Warden. Tell me what's so funny."

When I couldn't answer, his expression turned gleeful. "What? Cat got your tongue? If you think that's funny, then you'll love this." he growled, and then tossed me to the ground.

Well, that would imply a gentle little *plop*, when instead, it was more like a shot-put throw, the world swirling past my face at breakneck speed before I ate dirt.

First of all, rude. And second, ow.

I spat out forest bracken as I rolled to my side, my limbs taking forever to get with the program as I tried to suck in a breath. My ribs protested, my brain was mush, and just… *ow*. I hadn't quite managed to sit up before a boot the size of a fucking boat came at my face. I felt for my gun, the blessed thing still tucked into my spine holster, and had just enough time to draw it and shoot the offending foot before it made contact.

The ghoul howled, hopping on his lone uninjured foot as I scrambled to standing. The world picked that exact moment to start going hyper speed, whirling like a top while gravity decided to fuck off somewhere else. Stomach churning, world spinning, and jelly legged, I tried to focus.

Man, I was getting tired of concussions. Concussions pissed me off. And what had I done to this guy, huh? I was just driving here.

Squinting, I made out three other ghouls fighting alone with Jay, Jimmy, and a huge fucking grizzly bear.

Yazzie, you idiot.

Oh, right. Yazzie was a bear.

Yazzie, Yazzie was a bear…

In the middle of my Yazzie musings—which I probably should not have been doing in the middle of a ghoul fight, I know—a hand grabbed my shirt, lifting me off my feet. Again. Only this time, it was less to throw me across the forest in the worst game of Darby Frisbee ever, and more so the asshole could aim a punch at my face. Luckily, I was dealing with the dumbest ghoul in the history of ghouls because he forgot a very important detail.

I still had a gun in my hand.

At point-blank range—even with the mother of all concussions—I was a crack shot. Plus, his head was like, *right there*. Without hesitating, I fired, enjoying my victory for less than a second before his hand lost muscle control, and we fell right back down to the ground.

Considering this guy had to be close to eight feet, the drop was substantial. In a blissful stroke of luck, the ghoul managed to not land on me, but it was a near thing.

My smile was pure feral. "Who's laughing now, you prick?"

Shakily, I got to my feet, drawing my dagger. Ghouls couldn't just die from a bullet to the brain. He'd heal, and depending on how old he was, that healing could take minutes or hours.

Given my luck? I was going with minutes. Plus, I needed healing, and I'd take any soul at this point—even a greasy, grimy, pure-evil one if it meant I could help my friends.

I'd barely made it to the fallen ghoul before something slammed into my side, knocking me to the ground. My weapons went flying, my fingers losing muscle control as my ribs took the brunt of the blow. I was certain that the "something" was a boat-sized ghoul foot as a hand latched onto my hair and hauled me up.

Okay, it was one thing to wreck my Jeep. One thing to toss me around. But pulling my hair? That was just uncalled for.

My scalp was on fire as the sharp bite of pain lifted the fog from my brain. My hands began to glow as I shoved my power outward, knocking the both of us off-kilter. Ghouls were stronger than the majority of arcaners, faster than a track star, and harder to kill than weeds in summer.

But the one thing everyone needed—even ghouls —was air.

Just like I'd done with Astrid, I pressed that golden power into him, shoving the tendrils into his nose, his mouth, suffocating him for all I was worth. The only problem was that this form of offense was too slow.

Slow and ghouls did not mix.

He thrashed, my body following his movement like a rag doll since he still had ahold of my damn hair. I kicked, making that lovely connection with his balls, and the fucker finally let me go as he grabbed his junk and fell like a downed tree.

This time, I landed on my feet, my smile pure malice.

"See how you like *that*, fucker," I growled, hauling my foot back for another kick. I didn't care if I caught him in the balls again. I just wanted to connect with something. My boot caught his knee, the crunch of bone meeting my steel toe music to my ears.

The ghoul didn't so much as howl, all his air trapped in his lungs. Shoving my power down, I watched with glee as his face distorted from the pressure, his cheek smushing and his eyes popping wide.

But was pressing all I could do?

Back when Aemon had ahold of me, I'd been able to pick someone up and throw them. I wondered if I could do that again.

I imagined that golden light as an ethereal hand closing around the ghoul and hefting him up. Sure enough, he rose, but not high enough to do any damage. And the lifting, well...

Maybe experimenting with my abilities after a car wreck was a bad idea. Dizziness flooded me, and my knees started to buckle.

"A little help?" I mumbled. I'd tried to yell, but my thought process wasn't exactly working anymore.

My power flickered just as Yazzie bounded over, his

giant brown paws thudding against the ground with enough force to rattle my skull. Opening his jaws wide, he roared, showing his unbearably sharp teeth that could most definitely kill me if he had a mind for it.

I had to remember to not sing the "Yazzie, Yazzie was a bear" song. He'd probably eat me.

Those jaws latched onto the ghoul's head, ripping it from his shoulders with about as much fuss as my flicking a bug off my shoulder. Which was good since I was on my ass in the dirt, the weight of the wreck and overuse of power, causing my head to pour blood.

The cut I'd sustained in the crash was trickling blood into my eye, and my nose was acting up, and everything hurt and…

"Darby?" Jay murmured, squeezing my bicep. "You with me, babe?"

Wiping my nose, my hand came away bloody. "I'm a little fucked up."

"Yeah, I can see that. You want to take the souls?" he prompted gently, likely thinking I was brain damaged or something. He wasn't half wrong. "Get yourself back to rights?"

It wasn't a bad idea. But I worried that it would take too much time. What if there were more out there in the woods? What if more were waiting for us?

"Are there any more out there?" I asked, not even

trying to focus on his face. My brain felt like it was going to explode, and the world was spinning way too fast.

"Yep. That's why you need those souls—and pronto. Don't make me call for Hildy."

"Nooooooo," I moaned. Hildy would sass me and drain me even further. "Okay. I'll do it."

Focusing on the closest buzzing, I pulled the thread of the soul to me. Unwillingly he went, not wanting whatever afterlife was waiting for him. As soon as he touched me, I figured out why. As he healed me, I tossed my cookies on the forest floor, gasping for air as the wound in my scalp closed.

"Come on, D. You're still bleeding. Take more."

Tears in my eyes, I heaved again, but called the next soul. This one was far more eager to come to me, his spirit far cleaner, far less stained than his friend's had been.

His name was Ivan, and he'd only been a ghoul for a few years, taken from his bed at college one night. He'd never asked to be a member of the arcane and had been turned against his will. An unwilling member of the now-defunct Monroe nest, he tried to stay on the straight and narrow, but it was harder.

After the massacre at the lake, he left Tennessee—or at least he'd tried to. He'd gotten caught at the border, locked in a cage, and…

The rest was blank. It was as if his mind had been erased.

Who had the power to erase what was written on a soul? Who had the power to take everything a person was, and turn them into a killing machine? A good, honest kid was gone now because someone took their life from them.

It wasn't fair.

Opening my eyes, I realized the ache in my head was gone. My ribs still smarted, though, so that head wound had been a doozy. Honestly, at this point it was a wonder I *didn't* have brain damage.

"You need more, D," Jay ordered. "I am not getting my ass kicked by the Prince of Hell because you're too stubborn to heal up. Now hop to it."

Squinting, I focused on his face. Eyes red, fangs descended, Jay's expression was half-crazed. Shoulders tense, jaw locked, his hands were curled into the tufts of grass instead of touching me.

Oh. *Oh.*

I was covered in blood. From my hair all the way down to my toes. And Jay was new. He wanted me to heal up just in case I needed to fight, sure.

But what if the foe I needed to fight was him?

11

"Call another soul, Darby," Jay growled through gritted teeth, his entire body poised to strike. "Now."

My heart tripped double-time as I tried to assess just how screwed I was. Staring into those red eyes, I figured I was pretty fucked. Sure, Jimmy and Yazzie were here, but I'd seen a baby vamp go feral a time or two in my life and the results had never been pretty.

Hell, they were damn near barbaric.

Baby vamps didn't just drink their victims dry, they rent flesh, tearing their victims to pieces as they slurped them down. There wasn't a doctor in the world that could repair what a new vampire did to their prey, and I had no desire to bleed out after getting my ass kicked by a pack of ghouls.

Gulping a very dry swallow, my gaze never left Jay's as I called the last two souls. I barely saw the information each soul had to offer—I was too busy not moving, lest I triggered Jay. From what I did see, their lives before had been similar to Ivan's. Turned against their will, they were made into monsters and then their memories—their lives afterward—were just *gone*.

It reminded me of that poor soul at Whisper Lake. Lucas, I think his name was. He, too, had been turned against his will. He, too, had been plucked from his life and turned into a monster.

Against the covenant. Against the law. Against the natural order of things.

It was a problem I should have looked into sooner. I should have figured that poor ghoul caught in the middle of a war wasn't the only one that had been stolen.

And all the while, Jay's red eyes never left mine as he tried to hold himself back.

Was I going to have to put a bullet in my best friend?

I really fucking hoped not.

"How you holding up?" I murmured, trying not to spook the incredibly on edge, *very* new baby vamp.

"I'm ready to tear someone apart," Jay admitted, his body coiling, teeth grinding. "It's… it's overwhelming."

I'd never experienced bloodlust in the traditional

sense, so I couldn't possibly know exactly what he was feeling, but I knew *all* about wanting to tear someone apart.

I knew wanting to kill.

No one moved for one long moment, and then Jay was just *gone*.

His eyes blanked, his face going slack before hardening into this mindless thing that did not resemble my best friend at all. The red of his eyes bled all the way from his sclera to the tops of his cheekbones as blackened veins darkened his face. His fangs—which had already been out—lengthened further, the points sharper than a razor.

And the sound coming from his throat was straight out of a nightmare.

My best friend was going to kill me. Wasn't that just peachy?

Three things happened all at once. I rolled, flipping backward off my ass and landing on my knees, ready to run if I had to. Jay lunged, missing me by an inch as his growls grew feral. And Jimmy and the now human-shaped Yazzie pounced, grabbing onto my best friend as he snapped his teeth, summarily losing his shit.

Jay's fangs latched onto Yazzie's arm, and the shifter howled in outrage. That howl did nothing to dissuade him from his hunger. Jay shook his head like a rabid dog, tearing into Yazzie until the shifter hauled back and cold-cocked Jay right in the jaw. The blow snapped Jay's head up and back like a prize fighter, but my best friend was a fuck of a lot stronger than he'd been just days ago.

Stronger than a fully grown shifter.

All that hit did was piss Jay off.

He shoved, knocking Yazzie on his ass while he held onto Jimmy for dear life. Pulling Jimmy closer, he sniffed at the Fae, his snarls growing louder.

But he didn't strike—not yet.

"Come back to me," Jimmy whispered, reaching a trembling hand for Jay's cheek. "Find your way back to me, Jeremiah."

Jimmy was so much taller than us all, but I feared his size and know-how wasn't going to help him here. Not unless he wanted to use serious magic against his boyfriend. By the pained expression on Jimmy's face, I didn't know if he had it in him.

But if Jay was going to hurt Jimmy, I knew for a fact that he would want me to put him down by any means necessary. And I would, too.

A sparkling gold magic lit Jimmy's fingers as they touched Jay's cheek, the spell doing nothing for my best friend, the baby vamp. Jay's growls only got more guttural, more feral, his taloned fingers biting into Jimmy's arms.

Jimmy hissed in pain, and that was right about the time I decided to be done.

Enough of this shit.

My fingers patted the ground in search of a weapon since mine were off in the dirt somewhere, but all I found was a rock the size of a grapefruit.

That should do it.

Yanking that damn rock off the ground, I hauled back and chucked it right at Jay's stupid head. Jay and I had been protecting Jimmy Hanson since we were kids, and if he knew he was hurting his boyfriend, he'd launch himself off a cliff.

The rock slammed into Jay's temple, knocking him away from Jimmy just long enough for the elf to get free. Jay spun, snarling at me before he pounced once more, ready to tear me limb from limb.

Only, he never made it that far.

The thunder of a gunshot boomed right by my head, and Jay sailed backward, crumpling to the forest floor. The gun ratcheted, the unmistakable sound of a shotgun chambering a round making my whole body go cold for a second as my ears rang.

I so loved being deaf. It was my favorite.

Slowly, I turned, worried this was it, when a very familiar face had my whole body drooping in relief.

Sarina clucked her tongue at me as she surveyed my

bloody attire and dead-on-my-feet stance. "I swear to the Fates, I can't leave you alone for a minute, can I?"

I wanted to hug her. I also wanted to smack the shit out of her for blowing my fucking eardrum and shooting Jay, even though he'd totally deserved it. The same Jay who was groaning as Jimmy helped him sit up, eyes blue and fangs gone.

Okay, so maybe the smacking thing was unnecessary.

"You shot me with rock salt," Jay accused, picking bloody salt particles out of his shirt.

I'd thought I wanted to hug and smack Sarina—and I did—but Jay needed a kick in the nuts and hug so bad it wasn't funny.

"No, I shot you with *spelled* rock salt. You were about to snack on your friends. The spell and burn of the salt will keep you in check for a little while until you can get some food," Sarina shot back, resting the shotgun on her shoulder. "Why haven't you been eating, you blithering idiot? No blood for *days*. You won't drink from Jimmy, and you won't take a blood bag. Are you *trying* to kill people? Because *this* is how you kill people."

"I'm *fine*," Jay grumbled, and I had a hard time not knocking his stupid teeth out.

Yazzie did the thing I wanted to and slapped him upside the head. "Tell that to my fucking arm, you dick."

Jay's gaze fell onto the bloody tears at Yazzie's

shoulder and winced. Sure, the wound was healed already, but it had to have hurt like hell. "Sorry."

"Sorry *nothing*," Sarina scolded. "Get your shit together and get back to Ingrid's. I think the coast is clear, but I'm not seeing things like I should."

Sarina was an oracle. If she couldn't "see" something, things were about to get real fucking dicey, real fucking quick.

Perfect.

After a short search of the ground for my weapons and a forage through the wreck to get my bag, we set out to hike the last mile to Ingrid's home. Every sound in the woods seemed like a threat, so I didn't ask how Sarina had known where we were or what she was doing here.

Asking an oracle how she knew things was pointless, anyway.

Plus, Sarina and I hadn't parted on good terms when I'd left to return to the Warden house. Granted, that was probably my fault, but at least she wasn't saying sorry anymore, so there was that.

As soon as we crested the last ridge to Ingrid's, the bottom dropped out of my gut. I should have put two and two together. A pack of ghouls this close to the Enforcer of the Dubois nest's home? There was no way they were here for just me *if* they were here for me at all.

The back door to Ingrid's home stood wide open, the wood half off its hinges and windows smashed to oblivion. A bloody handprint streaked across the pale trim, highlighting just how late to the party we'd been.

A pair of feet were splayed across the threshold, the oversized shoes and puddle of blood not bringing good tidings.

It was so quiet. No shouts. No yells or signs of a battle. Maybe I was still deaf from the shotgun blast, but even the ringing had died.

Gun already drawn, Jay went in first, with me and Sarina in the middle, and Jimmy and Yazzie taking up the rear. Stepping over the large body of a rapidly decaying ghoul, I tried not to gag at the sheer level of carnage in the kitchen. Blood, body parts, and viscera blanketed the mosaic floors, the pattern lost under the dark pools.

Clearing each room, we came across more and more dead, and the ashes of the ancients. More blood. More viscera. Ghosts buzzed like bees nearby, their call just as deafening as the silence.

Shit.

Eyes tearing, I tried not to think the worst. I tried not to think of my small but mighty friend somewhere in these ashes. Ingrid's home. What if those ghouls were here for me? What if I brought this down on them?

In the room leading to the basement, a vampire hung, pinned to the wall by a stake in her chest. Curly black hair draped over her face as blood still dripped from her mouth. One of the younger vamps, she withered slightly, her desiccation slow. Her ghost, on the other hand, was strong.

Her grayed-out form raced for me, not stopping until she screamed in my face. "Where have you been?" she scolded, her name escaping me. "It was an ambush. There were so many. Too many."

"Getting my ass kicked by ghouls, same as you," I whispered, trying to keep my voice low. The house wasn't clear yet, and I didn't want to be surprised by a hulking freight train—especially considering I wasn't fully healed.

She stared pointedly at her desiccating body and then back to me. "Tell me about it. Have you found Ingrid?"

Eyes filling once more, I shook my head. There was no way to know whose ashes were whose.

"I think everyone is in the basement, but I can't get there," she said, pulling at one of her dark coils and twisting it around a finger as her shoulders drooped. "The place is warded against spells and ghosts. Björn was taking the baby vamps there for protection. Can you make sure they're okay?"

I nodded, ashamed I didn't know this girl's name.

"Do you want to pass?" I asked, holding out a hand. "I hear Elysium is nice this time of year."

"You'll help protect them, right? It was my job, but..." She trailed off, her dark eyes welling with silvery tears. "I failed."

"Of course I will, and you didn't fail."

Swallowing hard, she nodded and gave me her hand. Instantly, her name as well as a full life came to me. Valentina had been a vampire far longer than she had ever been a human. Attacked at the age of twenty, she'd been left for dead in the middle of a creek, her date having pitched her over the side of a bridge after he was done with her.

Mags found her. Turned her. Allowed her revenge, and then gave her a job to do. And since she'd been abused, she made it so no young vamp ever got hurt or hurt anyone else. Sixty years as a vampire, she'd helped so many find their feet in a new life.

That all ended when a ghoul rammed a stake through her heart.

And my biggest fear was that I'd find Ingrid the same damn way.

12

"There's movement in the basement," Jay breathed as he grabbed my bicep and dragged me behind him. "I need your head in the game."

There was nothing I hated more than when Jay went into BFF protector mode. But right now, my head was not in the game, my heart was broken for the woman I'd just absorbed, and I was really fucking scared that someone else I cared about could possibly be dead.

I'd lost so much already. It wasn't fair. None of this was fair.

Gritting my teeth, I shoved his hand off my arm. "I'm fine. Björn and the baby vamps fled to the basement. It's probably them, but keep your eyes peeled."

Valentina's life weighed heavily on my heart. She'd

only been eighty—such a short life for a vampire. Maybe it was the flashes of Ingrid's care of her, maybe it was how she cared for others, but her story resonated with me in a way that had me craving vengeance on her behalf.

Jay's expression screwed up in his "I'm worried about you" face but I elected to ignore it. I wasn't the one who'd almost munched on my best friend. He could worry about himself.

Slowly, Jay opened the basement door, the well-oiled hinges making nary a peep. Silently, we descended the stone steps, the narrow walls seeming to close in around us as we waited for something to jump out at us. But it wasn't until we got to the bottom of the steps and fanned out amongst the arched cells did anything make a move.

Granted, the *only* thing to make a move was fucking Astrid, but whatever. Her pale arm shot from the cell bars, latching onto Sarina's wrist and scaring the absolute fuck out of everyone. Hell, the bitch almost got shot.

"Thank the Fates," she said on a sigh before her face twisted into a scowl. "What took you so long? I could have been stuck in this cell forever."

Two things registered in my brain at once. One, I hated Astrid with every fiber of my being, and if I could catapult her into the sun, it would only be a benefit to the world at large.

And two? Astrid had gotten the jump on Sarina.

I ignored the screeching witch in favor of staring the small oracle down, her brown eyes filled with an odd sort of shame that made no sense to me.

"We're going to talk about this later," I murmured before directing my attention to Astrid. "Shut. Up."

If we'd ever had the element of surprise, it was long gone now. I gave Jay the signal and we moved quickly, not caring about silence as we cleared the rest of the basement. The only place left to check out was an old closet that couldn't possibly hold all the young vampires and Jay's maker.

Jay splayed his hand against the wood, a faint trace of a smile flitting across his lips. Unbidden, he rapped against the door in the standard "Shave and a Haircut" bit. The answering two knocks made him breathe a sigh of relief.

I saved my relief until the door opened wide and a *remarkably* familiar bald head peered out of the open space. Björn's expression was a step just past feral, his eyes wide as he checked Jay over.

"You lost it. I felt you lose it," Jay's maker rumbled, his giant hands latching onto Jay's shoulders and shaking him a little. "I swore up and down you were fine, and you do this shit? Why haven't you been drinking? Why have you been lying to me? *How* are you lying to me?"

Jay shrugged. "I was fine until this one," he said, hooking a thumb at me, "decided to damn near bleed to death. And I wasn't lying. I thought I was fine."

Okay, first of all, I didn't decide shit. Second, if he wanted to keep working with me, he needed to eat. Hell, especially if he wanted to work with me.

"Sure," Björn huffed, rolling his eyes. "And I'm the Easter Bunny." Then the big man's gaze searched us, his eyes hardening when they fell on me. "Where's Ingrid?"

It seemed the bottom of my gut was a trap fucking door because it fell away again, that sick, trembling dread nearly making me ill. I shook my head. "I don't know."

Björn shouldered the rest of the way out of the closet —a closet that was not a closet at all, but a tunnel system that I had no interest in exploring—and shoved his way through us.

He didn't say a word as he hauled ass up the stairs, but Jay and I followed hot on his heels back through the house of horrors and ghoul guts. Björn stopped so fast, both Jay and I ran into him, skidding through puddles of gross and nearly biffing it in the kitchen. I curled around the big man to see the threat, only to almost fall to my knees in relief.

Well, not to my knees—because *gross*—but you get the picture.

A very tiny, very bloody, red-eyed Ingrid stood in the kitchen doorway, a desiccating severed head hanging by the hair in her fist. Her left eye was twitching as she ground her teeth, her rage filling the room like a cloud of poison.

I opened my mouth to ask a question—what, I didn't know—but a lone raised finger stopped me. Ingrid shook her head before heading straight to the refrigerator. She reached into the cold storage and yanked out three blood bags and popped them in the microwave. Then she ripped open the freezer, unearthing a bottle of vodka.

With a single thumb, she screwed off the top of the bottle and started downing it like someone was going to ban booze soon. I knew Ingrid was older than Jesus himself, but watching her tiny childlike body guzzle vodka like a sorority sister at a kegger made me mighty uncomfortable.

When the microwave beeped after a very long minute of straight drinking, she tilted her head back down and slammed the nearly empty bottle onto the counter.

"Ing? Baby girl?" I cooed, a little afraid of my pissed-off friend. "You need some help?"

Her body didn't move, but she did turn her head, spearing me with a look so full of venom, it was a wonder I was still standing.

"No," she growled, dropping the severed head from her fingers, and unearthing the blood bags from the microwave.

It was tough not to be worried about her at that moment, especially when she ripped through a bag like it was a personal affront. A moment later, the first bag was gone, and in the next, as was the second. The third bag she tossed at Jay.

Well, maybe "tossed" was the wrong word. That implied that she didn't rocket it at him like a fucking fastball. She swiped the vodka bottle from the counter, kicked the head with enough force to embed it into the next wall, and hopped up on the counter to have herself a seat.

Jay managed to catch the bag, but he didn't rip into it like she had. No, he just stared at the blood encased in plastic like he'd never seen one before.

"*Drink,*" Ingrid ordered, putting a fair amount of influence into the command. Hell, her compulsion damn near made me want to find a tall glass of *whatever* and start chugging.

I didn't know if an ancient like Ingrid could use her mind mojo on younger vamps, but it seemed like she sure was going to try.

Reluctantly, Jay pulled the plastic tab at the top and put it to his mouth. As soon as that first taste hit his tongue, Jay started devouring it, pouring it down his throat as fast as he could swallow.

Eyes red, fangs out, he tore into the poor plastic like his life depended on it. I knew where this was going. Rolling my eyes, I went to the fridge. I seriously doubted Jay would care whether his blood was cold or not, and I didn't want him to start snacking on me.

This time when a bag was tossed in his direction, he tore into it without the least bit of hesitation, sucking it dry before I had time to blink. I tossed him a third and fourth, and by the time a fifth landed in his hands, a sleepy sort of contentment filled his expression as he leisurely drank it down.

When Jay was done, he let out an almighty belch, and then his shoulders finally climbed out of his ears, and his jaw unclenched.

"You know what you feel right now?" Björn asked, his gaze and voice like a disappointed god. "That is 'not hungry.' Before? Hungry. Now? Not hungry. Just like I told you yesterday after you told me you ate, you need three to seven bags a day as a newbie. Lying to me is going to get us both killed. Got it?"

Jay's sheepish expression pulled at my heartstrings,

but as much as it hurt that he was adjusting to this new normal, I couldn't help myself. Like any best friend would, I marched across that kitchen, and flicked him right on the nose.

Okay, so I picked my way through body parts, but whatever.

"How many times have I been right in the forever we've known each other?"

Jay sighed and hung his head. "Too many to count."

Stowing my gun, I narrowed my eyes. "When have I ever been wrong?"

That was a ballsy question for me to ask, especially after Bishop, but I sallied forth, ignoring the memory of the mage wholeheartedly.

"Never." At least he answered the way he always had since we were twelve, and I'd proven him so wrong he almost cried.

The tips of my lips lifted, the small bit of normalcy a balm to my shattered nerves. "What are you going to do?"

Jay actually stomped his foot, though it was in a blood puddle, and I was pretty sure he squished some brain matter with his boot.

Gross.

"Listen to you," he answered, crossing his arms over his chest.

Nodding, I dismissed him for the tiny vamp who'd polished off the vodka. "What in the unholy fuck happened here?"

Rolling her eyes, she hopped off the counter to rummage in the freezer. She unearthed another bottle, though this time, it was gin. "What do you think happened? Do you see any heads around here?" She twisted off the lid and took a sip. "Ghoul attack. Obviously. One plus one equals two, bitch."

Personally, I thought the "bitch" comment was unnecessary, but since she was peeved—and two thousand years older than me—I decided to allow it.

"I had to hunt three of those fuckers down after they ran. Three. They thought they could outrun me. Thought they could hide out in the forest, and I wouldn't smell them. It's like they didn't know who they were going up against."

Considering the sheer size of the blank spots in the ghouls' souls, I would be willing to bet they didn't have that first clue. No, this had been a distraction. A big one. But for what? "Any get away?"

Ingrid huffed a mirthless laugh and took another swig. She ran a bloody hand over her mouth, swiping at a drop of gin and smearing the red further. "Nope. I got them all. Fuck of a lot of good it did me. Val is still dead, my house has been invaded, and it looks like I can't even keep your wayward ass safe." She raised her bottle in a mock-cheers. "Gold stars all around."

"They say why they came? What they wanted?" Because unless she had even the slightest bit of insight, I had no idea why a pack of ghouls just decided to fuck shit up on a random Wednesday. My gut said distraction, but honestly, I didn't know anymore.

Ingrid sipped her booze, staring at me like I was three marbles short of a full bag. "No again. Just busted in and started ripping shit apart."

Super. I so love dead ends. They're my favorite.

"Did Shiloh get anything out of Astrid at least?" I asked, kind of put out that all the chairs were broken, and I couldn't take a load off like I wanted.

Speaking of, where was Shiloh? I hadn't seen either her or Acker, and unless they were with the baby vamps in the tunnels…

Ingrid's frown had my gut hopping on the fucking trap door again. Or maybe it was because she put down the booze. "What are you talking about? Shiloh left with you."

Slowly, I nodded. "Yeah, and then she left the crime scene before I did to question Astrid about the missing witches. Acker went with her. They were headed back *here*."

Ingrid shook her head. "I hate to break it to you, babe, but they didn't make it."

Taking in the sheer amount of viscera around me, I had to wonder if this was a good or *unbelievably* bad thing.

13

Without another word, I ran back downstairs to the basement, searching for Sarina. Finding her in a sea of young vampires, I latched onto her arm and dragged her back up the stairs.

Sarina squawked in protest, but that didn't stop me from yanking her out from under the wards that protected the basement. There was a fair amount of shit I wanted to ask her, but it started with why she was here, how she knew where we were, and what the fuck was going on with her powers.

But all of that was far less important than where Shiloh was.

"Shiloh's missing. I want you to find her." No, I

didn't say please, and no, I didn't ask nice. Nice was a luxury I didn't have.

Sarina pulled her arm out of my grip and took a healthy step back. "What do you mean she's missing? I thought she was in Georgia with her cousin."

It was weird having to fill the oracle in on anything at all. Hell, usually, even my thoughts weren't safe. And they hadn't been until Jimmy put that amulet around my neck. I'd had a sneaking suspicion that Jimmy's amulet kept everything out, even tiny telepaths like Sarina.

"She came back yesterday. Witches are missing. She thinks it's Nero."

Though, until I had proof he was actually here, I would be saving my worry. Trust me, I had enough to spare.

"Shiloh left a crime scene before I did to come talk to Astrid, and she never showed up. Probably lucky since we damn near got ripped apart in a ghoul attack, but—"

Sarina pinched her brow. "You need to know where she is." She sighed long and low like she was gearing up for something, a something I probably would not like. "I can't help you."

Yep. Don't like it one bit.

Was I glad she'd showed up when we needed her? Absolutely.

Was I tiptoeing toward rage now that she couldn't help? Yeah, a little.

"And why can't you help me?" I asked, forcing my voice into a calm, low tone so I wouldn't start screaming.

Rolling her eyes, she hooked a finger into the collar of her shirt, unearthing an amulet on a long chain. An amulet that appeared strikingly similar to mine.

"What did you do? Moreover, what does *that* do?" I demanded, pointing a sharp finger at the stone.

The giant garnet at my throat kept all spells that did harm from sticking. It also protected my mind. Well, that part hadn't been confirmed, but I suspected it did.

Sarina's jaw hardened as she tucked the necklace back under her shirt. "It does exactly what it is supposed to, but unlike you, it also affects my abilities. I used to think I wanted to be blind like this, but…"

She shook her head and pivoted on a heel, stomping back down the steps. A moment later, she emerged from the stairs with Jimmy in tow. I had to wonder *why* she wanted an amulet like mine—or at least I did until I remembered that I hadn't been the only one that Bishop had spelled.

Bishop La Roux was a powerful mage. In fact, he was so powerful that I couldn't be sure what the limits of his abilities even were. He was ruthless, cunning, and—

worst of all—crazier than a shit house rat. He'd hidden so much from the both of us, but Sarina was the one who felt guilty.

"You're going after him, aren't you?" I murmured, my whole body going cold. Not that I didn't want her help—I did. But Bishop was far smarter than I'd given him credit for, and he'd managed to keep more than he should from Sarina.

"You think you've cornered the market on revenge? I worked with that man for longer than you've been alive. He was my *friend*." Tears welled up in her dark eyes. "One of the few I actually had. But every bit of it was a lie. Everything. All the way down to investigating you. I helped him, Darby. I helped him hurt you, and I thought I was doing the right thing."

I couldn't imagine being duped for that long. Couldn't begin to understand just how she felt, but my empathy didn't matter. Sarina, without her power, was more vulnerable than I was by a long shot.

"You didn't know," I murmured, wanting to reach for her but unable to make myself. A part of me still saw Bishop when I looked at her, and that bit of shame that came along with it was still there between us.

Her expression turned bitter. "You're right. I didn't know. Some oracle I turned out to be, right?" She swiped at her eyes, dashing tears off her cheeks. "I didn't know, and he damn near killed us all. That's why I need this thing off." Shooting a dark look over her shoulder at Jimmy, she lifted the chain from her shirt. "The damn thing won't even let me lift it over my head."

I'd cursed the necklace, too, when I'd first gotten it. I sang a different tune after Bishop failed to take it off me in the caves. There was no way to fully thank Jimmy for that necklace, no way to truly tell him just how much he'd saved me.

"You don't want me to do that," he replied, skirting around us both as he headed toward the kitchen.

Like the puppies we were, Sarina and I followed him.

"And why is that?" Sarina hissed. "I can't see shit with this fucking thing on. Astrid snuck up on me, I can't find Bishop, and I barely made it in time to save you from an anorexic vampire. I think I know what I want, Jimmy."

"Hey," Jay protested around a straw poked into a new blood bag. "I'm eating."

Sarina, Ingrid, and I all stared at Jay and his blatant bullshit, but Sarina was the one to dress him down. "After you attacked your friend and bit a colleague. Sure. You're the picture of healthy boundaries."

Jay frowned and went back to his juice box, grumbling something about never being able to live it down or whatever.

"I need my powers back," Sarina insisted, planting her fists on her hips. "If I would have known they were going to be muted, I would have never put the fucking thing on."

Jimmy winced. "It's going to give you a headache. And maybe make you a teensy bit crazy." Hunching his shoulders, the big man grimaced. "And maybe knock you out for a day or three."

"What the fuck, Jimmy?"

I mean, come on. None of us had time to deal with the ramifications of Sarina taking that damn necklace off. We were standing in ghoul guts with a missing witch and agent...

Digging in my bag, I found my phone. Acker could be tracked. Dialing Tobin, I shot Jimmy a scowl.

"What?" he hissed. "She was half-crazy to begin with, and this is the first time she hasn't had a headache in fifty years. Excuse the fuck out of me for wanting to give her a break."

"Boundaries, dude. Boundaries," Björn said, shaking his head.

Four rings later—and a fair bit of anxiety—Tobin finally answered.

"Yeah?" he said, half out of breath if his wheezing was any clue. What the fuck had he been doing?

"Please tell me you can track Acker." I gave him the rundown of the situation to Tobin's utter silence.

"Tobin?" I prompted, my unease mounting with each quiet second. "Aldrich?"

He sniffed, the wet sound doing nothing to make my unease go away. Tobin was on top of everything. He was practically salivating to help, the urge to be accepted his driving force.

"If you're in trouble, say 'You got it, boss,' and I'll come, okay? You need me, and I'm there."

He sucked in a pained breath, a little whimper escaping his lips. "Y-you g-got it, b-boss."

Oh, fuck. Oh fuck, oh, shit, oh, no.

"I'm coming, okay," I insisted, meeting Yazzie's eyes as he shouldered into the room. "I'm coming."

Even though I didn't want to, I ended the call, shifting to face Ingrid. "I need keys."

Hildy, I need you. Now.

Ingrid nodded, raced to her office, and returned with a key fob in hand. "Here. Take it. It's the big black SUV in the garage."

She tossed the keys to me, and I caught them midair as Hildy's grayed-out form appeared in the kitchen.

"What's goin' on, lass?" He surveyed the damage of the room, eyes wide as he took in the sheer carnage. "Seriously, what the fuck happened?"

I didn't have the time to explain the intricacies of just how fucked we all were and reduced it down to "Ghoul attack." What the fuck else was I going to say?

"Well, I didn't think ya were playin' Go Fish. What I wanna know is why you're half-dead on your feet, and there isn't a ghost in this place. How hurt are ya, lass?"

Leave it to Hildy to bring up even more shit I didn't have time to think about.

Did I care about the utter lack of ghoul ghosts? *Yep.*

Did Tobin have that kind of time? *Absolutely not.*

"That's not why I called you. I think someone is holding Tobin hostage at the house. Considering our ghost problem, I want you to *carefully* scope it out and report back. This has 'trap' written all over it."

Hildy's eyes narrowed, his jaw clenching, as his skull cane began to glow.

Oh, great. He's winding up to give me a lecture. I so have time for this.

"What I wanna know is why you're acting like you don't matter. That your health doesn't matter."

Spinning on a heel, I headed for the garage. "You gonna help me or not, old man? I have a guy probably hurt. One is missing. Shiloh is in the wind. I've been attacked by ghouls, my Jeep is totaled, and a boatload of witches are missing. Give me a fucking break, would ya?"

That didn't even account for the dead witch ghost bombs going off. What the fuck was happening in my neck of the woods? Was it an apocalypse, and no one told me?

"Fine," he said with a sigh as I beeped the locks on the SUV and slid into the driver's seat. "But when I come back, don't jump like you're prone to. Can't have ya wrecking two cars, now, can we?"

My eye twitched, and I honestly contemplated telling him to fuck off, but I didn't. The absolute last thing I needed was for him to actually do it. I did, however, shoot him a look so venomous his mirth fled.

"I said, 'fine.' But if it is a trap, you'd better be callin' in more reinforcements." Then he popped out of sight as if his word were law and needed no response from me.

All at once, the passenger doors opened, half-scaring me out of my seat. Yazzie took the front, Jay, Jimmy, and Sarina in the middle row, and Björn in the back. I didn't even ask why the big man had decided to tag along. I was just glad for the backup.

A part of me didn't like that Jay was behind me, his spot taken by the shifter, but the other part didn't really care who was coming, as long as they were able-bodied and ready to get bloody if need be.

"First things first," Sarina said as I pressed the

ignition and the garage door button. "I need this damn necklace off. I need to be able to see, Jimmy. Now."

I backed out of the garage as soon as the SUV would clear the door and peeled out of the courtyard while Sarina and Jimmy bickered in the backseat.

And that's about when Yazzie had enough.

"Get it done," he growled. And not that sound men do when they're pissed. No, the sound coming out of Yazzie's throat was all animal, and a quick glance to the side had me gripping the steering wheel in a white-knuckled grip just so I didn't pee my pants.

The agent was half-shifted in the passenger seat of this damn SUV. Sure, it was nice and roomy, but I seriously doubted it could hold all eight hundred pounds of a pissed-off bear.

"You have five seconds to get that fucking necklace off her before I rip you both out of this car. If you can't help, you're dead weight, and I don't need you. That's my friend in that house. Tobin is *my friend*. And he's scared and alone and probably hurt. So, get your shit together or get out of this car."

I met Jimmy's gaze for just a moment in the rearview mirror. He didn't want to hurt Sarina, and he knew he was going to.

"Okay, but when she passes out—and she will—remember you told me to do this."

Gold magic lit the cab like a new sun had been formed in his hand, and he snapped his fingers. A moment later, Sarina's scream ripped through the air, nearly making me slam on the brakes. Then her screams abruptly cut off, which had me glancing back at the oracle.

Sarina—just like Jimmy had warned—was passed out in the Fae's arms. I caught the blood darkening her nostrils and her pale skin before I had to put my eyes back on the road. Flooring it, I raced down the street, trying to keep my cool.

"She breathing?" I didn't want to ask that question, but I had to. "What's going on?"

"She's breathing," Jimmy answered begrudgingly. "But she's bleeding from the nose. You all happy now?"

"We're not the ones who took her powers away in the first place." Björn's rumble sounded from the far back. "You know what you did is wrong. Don't shovel the blame away just because you feel bad about it now."

"You don't know, man," Jimmy countered. "She came to me bawling. Ranting about how her powers were useless and that she shouldn't be able to see. She said she needed protection from Bishop. She said..." He trailed off, the hurt in his voice breaking my heart. "She didn't know what she was asking for, but I gave it to her, anyway. Yeah, I fucked up, but she asked for my help. What was I going to say? No?"

Two minutes later—which seemed like an eternity, but whatever—Hildy popped into the car, scaring me half to death.

I didn't drive off the road, but it was close.

"I have bad news for ya, lass," he began, his words yanking the trap door of my gut once again.

"Trap?" I croaked, getting myself under control.

Hildy nodded, meeting my gaze in the rearview.

"Trap."

14

While Hildy enumerated just how fucked the situation we were walking into was, I navigated the city streets of Knoxville like I had a siren on top of this car. Granted, the absolute last thing I needed was a cop trying to stop me as I traversed into the arcane side of town, but I couldn't exactly slow down.

"You wanna clue the rest of us in?" Yazzie barked, irritated at my one-sided conversation.

Well, I didn't care for it too much either, but thems were the breaks.

"Hildy can't get into the house. Whoever's there has put wards up to keep all ghosts out. Dark ones." There were only so many types of arcaners who could do something like that. Death mages being at the tippy top of that list.

I didn't have the juice to just walk in there if Bishop was in that house. Not after last time. He'd beaten me. He won. Without Aemon's help, I would have died in those caves just like he'd wanted me to. Bishop killed Essex and Davenport—not that either were missed— he'd nearly taken Jay from me.

And none of that even scratched the surface of all the truth and trauma I'd stuffed down deep so I wouldn't have to think about it. The lies. The violation. The horrific uncertainty of not knowing what was real and what had been a spell.

Not to mention, I didn't... *I couldn't* face him again... Not unless I was positive I would win. Clenching my jaw, I found a parking lot and pulled over, slamming the big SUV into "Park" before it was fully stopped.

Gripping the steering wheel, I let out the scream that had been bubbling in my gut for some time. I wasn't ready. I didn't have enough weapons. Didn't have enough power. I wanted Bishop dead so bad. Wanted him to hurt, to know the pain he inflicted on so many other people. On me.

But I wasn't. Fucking. Ready.

And I didn't think I could call Sloane, not when she hadn't answered before, and I didn't know where

Bastian and Thomas were, and Astrid was no help, and Shiloh was missing, and...

Bastian and Thomas. They could help, right?

But what if it wasn't Bishop? What if it was someone else? What if it was whoever killed that girl in the National Cemetery? What if—

"Fates above, I'm up," Sarina croaked. "No need to burst my eardrums. Aww, man. Am I bleeding?" She seemed affronted at the very thought of a nosebleed.

Twisting in my seat, I breathed a truncated sigh of relief. I was so happy she was with us, but my relief was minimal at best. There was just too much up in the air.

Yazzie popped the glove compartment and handed her a packet of tissues.

"Dammit, Jimmy. You weren't wrong about that headache. Anyone got any aspirin?" She rubbed at the side of her head. "I forgot how loud everything is."

Digging through my messenger bag, I unearthed a bottle of pain reliever and passed it over. We didn't have any water, though, so she'd have to dry-swallow them.

Squinting one eye, she studied my face. "I still can't read your thoughts, but your face says bad things." She shifted to face Jimmy. "Did you build that into the necklace, or am I brain damaged?"

Jimmy huffed a short laugh, pulling her into a hug.

"It's in the necklace. No one but Sloane can hear her now."

Snorting, I shot her a hard look. "Hildy can't get into the house."

Sarina immediately sat up, wincing as she went. "You think it's Bishop."

Nodding, I rotated forward in my seat and put the SUV back in "Drive." I did think it was Bishop. But when it came to him, I couldn't trust my gut anymore. Bishop was the boogeyman in all the dark corners of my brain. He was everywhere.

I would always think it was him. I would always wonder if he was around the next corner. I would always fear that every single memory I had where he was concerned was another spell, another lie, another trick.

Until I killed him, Bishop would haunt me worse than any ghost.

"It's not him," she murmured, her reassurance weak at best. "Jimmy tuned the wards so he couldn't come in, right?"

That didn't mean a lick of good if someone had altered them, now, did it?

That meant she had to be guessing then. *Fabulous.* "You can't see inside the house, can you?"

"I can, too," she insisted, her lip curling in affront. "I just can't see *him*. He could be there, but he could also be in Nepal in an ashram with the fucking monks for all I know. I don't know what kind of mojo Essex put on him, but seeing his future hasn't been a picnic. Like *ever*. Mostly, I focus on the people around him. Unfortunately, I don't know who he's with, so finding him is a bit of an issue right now."

Eye twitching, I blew through a red light to the chorus of honks.

"Maybe focus that third eye on the very scared agent, then?" Yazzie growled, his irritation not backing down an inch. "You know, the one who is stuck hurt and alone and without any fucking backup. Can you do that?"

The sigh that came out of Sarina told me she was having none of Yazzie's attitude. "And like I said. Bishop's not in the house. As far as I can see, only Tobin is there. He's breathing. Beat up, but alive." She drew that last word out for a second like she was not quite sure she was telling the truth. "Wait. What the fuck is *that*?"

Less than a mile from the house, I parked on the street and surveyed the tiny oracle as she rubbed her temple, a crumpled, bloody tissue in her hand.

She shook her head. "There's *someone* there, but I can't see them. It's like they're blurry or something. Like someone went into my sight and tried to delete them."

Again, not. Comforting.

"The best I can tell you is that there are two, I think." Sarina squinted as if she was trying to see through blurry glasses. "Both blonde, small, and definitely arcane."

Well, I didn't think they were gonna be the fucking Tooth Fairy.

I managed to keep that quip to myself, but it was very close to falling out of my mouth, and I'd never been so happy she could not read my mind.

Two small, blonde arcaners with the ability to hide from Sarina and keep all ghosts out of my house?

And we were walking in blind.

Super.

Hildy was right. We did need more backup.

"Thomas is on his way. He says to give him five," Björn announced from the third row, his tone hopeful if resolute. "He's bringing Bastian and Dahlia with him."

"We don't *have* five," Yazzie snarled, opening his door and climbing from the car.

How he managed to do that with whatever human-bear amalgamation he was rocking, I didn't know, but I sure as shit wasn't going to ask him. I was just glad we were on the arcane side of town and that he hadn't fully shifted into a bear. Knoxville was Tennessee through and through, but an eight-hundred-pound bear would cause a stir no matter what side of town we were on.

Everyone piled out of the SUV—including Sarina, who had no business going anywhere except to bed to sleep for a week. My face must have said as much because she flipped me off and strode after Yazzie, trying to catch up to him on her short legs.

Latching onto her shoulder, I yanked her to a stop. "Where the fuck do you think you're going?"

She shrugged off my hand, her blistering glare not making me back down an inch. "I'm getting real tired of you thinking you can tell me what to do. I'm not a pet you get to trot out when you need something. I'm a real-live person with actual thoughts in my brain and everything."

No, she did not get to pull that pity party bullshit with me.

"And I'm getting real tired of you thinking you can walk into a dangerous situation with no gun, no armor, no energy, *and* hurt. You know damn well you aren't a pet or a possession. If you could see inside my mind right now, you'd know that I'm worried about you. But fuck me, right? Fuck our friendship and every bit of history we've had up until you couldn't reassure yourself constantly that I'm not a monster."

Sarina's face fell, her jaw working overtime as she clenched and unclenched it in what looked like an effort to shut up.

"Stay at the back, do not get within a block of that house, and take this," I ordered, passing over my dagger. I didn't want to give it up, but her shotgun was nowhere to be found, and she couldn't go anywhere empty-handed.

There were quite a few caches of weapons around the house, and if I could get to them, I'd be fine.

In theory.

Not waiting for her to get her head out of her ass, I spun on a heel and raced after Yazzie. At about a block away from the Warden house, he got off the main drag and started cutting through the back alley where we put our trash bins on Tuesdays.

I was just glad he decided to be smart and not go through people's backyards. On the human side of town? That was fine. But here? It was a good way to cross a ward and get your ass fried.

Four doors down, I caught sight of the turret that was my bedroom, the lavender scalloped shingles peeking through the elm tree that shaded the backyard half the day. Thankfully, Yazzie slowed to a crawl, allowing me to catch up.

"What's the plan here?" I whispered, not wanting any sort of arcaner to overhear us. Who the fuck knew who my neighbors were? I sure as shit didn't.

"I suppose I can watch the exits," Hildy offered, his

mouth screwed up in chagrin. "I hate that I can't watch your back, lass."

Me, too, Hild. Me, too.

"Good idea. Hildy said he'd watch the back so no one escapes. We have to assume whoever is in there will know when we cross their new wards, so—"

"Standard breach formation?" Jay said, finishing my sentence.

Nodding, I checked the mag on my Glock and chambered a round. "There are three caches of weapons on the first floor. In the island cabinet, in the wardrobe on the first-floor guest room, and in the China cabinet in the dining room. I only have thirteen rounds left, so I'm going to the first one I can reach."

"I'm going for Tobin," Yazzie growled, "but I don't need anything else."

"I'm set," Jimmy said, pulling a sword from thin air.

Jay chambered a round and gave me a nod, and Björn just cracked his knuckles before pulling his filigreed wand from the breast pocket of his leather jacket. Okay, we were as ready as we were ever going to be.

The standard breach formation basically put a man on every usable doorway, and all units breached the space at once in a snare tactic that hadn't failed us yet. Though, not once had we breached a building where we were dealing with arcaners that had enough juice to keep Hildy out.

"You aren't starting the party without us, are you?" Bastian called, his approach damn near silent as the grave. Thomas and Dahlia were right behind him, their arrivals just as quiet.

Bastian tutted at me like I was a naughty child before tossing me a bulletproof vest. "Sloane told me to tell you to put that on. She also said she was not amused with your antics thus far, and you two were going to have a 'discussion' of some kind. I would be very wary of her use of that word. When she and I have a 'discussion,' I'm usually in trouble."

Grumbling, I strapped the black tactical vest over my still-bloody shirt. Honestly, if she wanted to scold me via a third party, she could just shove it. What the fuck was I supposed to do? Huh? Not get attacked by ghouls? Stop investigating murders? Let the city of Knoxville cannibalize itself?

None of this had been my fault. I was just trying to do my job and breathe for a second and the whole world decided to just fall to shit.

"How about if she has something to say to me, she can say it to my fucking face? Maybe she can come here herself instead of sending in the 'B' team. *Maybe* a bulletproof vest isn't going to do diddly squat against literally any arcaner ever." Dismissing him, I met everyone's eyes one by one. "We're going in standard breach, one team on every door. Jimmy, you give us the signal?"

Jimmy gave me a reassuring smile. "Yes, ma'am. I'll see if the warding that keeps Hildy out needs cracking."

"I'll help," Dahlia added, and the pair took off toward the house.

Yazzie gave everyone a rundown of the entrances, and we were off, following Jimmy and Dahlia to the back gate, staying low just in case someone was watching.

By the time we got into position behind the back gate, Jimmy and Dahlia were buzzing like bees.

"It's a trap," Dahlia insisted. "There is nothing stopping a breach. All the wards I saw when I came here yesterday are gone. Nothing to keep out anyone but the dead. It's like they want us to come in."

And that's when Yazzie lost it, a growl ripping up his throat like the bear he was. "Tobin is in there. If you want to be scared in the alley, fine, but I'm going in."

In a blink, the half-shifted man went from two legs to four, the gray mist of his change making all of us back up. A moment later, he was up and over the six-foot privacy fence, as if gravity were a mere notion that he'd decided to ignore.

Shit.

I—along with everyone else—scrambled after the giant fucking bear, losing the element of surprise, losing any leverage, losing every single bit of cool I might have actually had. I followed the fucking moron into the house, gun drawn, ready to defend the idiot if need be.

But Sarina had been wrong, her sight failing her far more than she knew. Because there weren't just *two* small, blonde arcaners holed up in the Warden house.

There was an army of them.

15

I t was the hesitation that fucked me.

There was a very good reason Ingrid was so effective when heading into battle. Most people, when faced with a kid, would hesitate—their innate need to protect someone seemingly weaker, making them unable to harm their opponent.

It was how she got the upper hand in most fights. Because who else but a monster would hurt a child?

As soon as Yazzie bounded through that door, busting it off its hinges, and I saw what was on the other side? It took a long second to figure out just how fucked we were.

A second that we absolutely did not have.

With limited ammo, no dagger, and dwindling power, we weren't just fucked. We were *fucked*.

A fine-boned young man, maybe no more than fifteen or sixteen, stood in the middle of the kitchen, his sickly pale face pulled into an innocent expression. He wore a suit like a little adult, his hair molded to his head with enough gel to choke a goat. The dark circles beneath his eyes veined out to the top of his cheeks, making the bright-red irises and sclera shine like beacons.

Behind him were four carbon copies, their blond hair and pale skin gleaming under the bright light of the kitchen chandelier.

Yazzie didn't hesitate like I had, he went right for the boy in front, swiping at him with his giant bear paw. The problem lay in the fact that not only was the boy not alone, but he was *fast*.

Ingrid fast.

As much as the world slowed when I had a gun in my hand, as much power as I had at my disposal, I just wasn't fast enough. Yazzie's swipe missed by a mile as the kid let out a creepy little, tinkling bell laugh—the same laugh that was echoed by the identical boys right behind him.

Then I registered just how old he was.

The buzz of his life force rattled my brain the same way all old ones did, the time etched in their souls vibrating the very air around them.

Yazzie either didn't register the danger or he just didn't give a shit. His failed swipe didn't seem to matter to him one bit. He stood on his hind legs, his roar rattling the windows as he reached out his claws for another pass.

The boy in front practically pirouetted around the bear, his laugh chilling me to the bone—especially when a moment later it echoed from the other boys' mouths. And then he was in front of me, so fast I never even got a shot off.

"We've been waiting for you," he said, his voice deeper than I'd thought it would be, and with an accent I couldn't place. Slavic maybe, or Germanic, or maybe someplace older that I'd never even heard of before. "Too bad you brought the vermin with you."

Yazzie's roar was quickly cut off when the boy shot out an arm, slamming into the bear with the back of his hand with enough force to knock the shifter through the kitchen wall. Granted, it was the part of the wall where the door stood, so the impact was enough to shake the entire house.

And he did it without moving his gaze even the slightest millimeter from mine.

His silent friends didn't so much as twitch either, their blank stares reminding me of dolls.

Gripping my gun, I contemplated if this asshole was faster than a bullet. Unfortunately, I figured the answer was solidly in the affirmative column.

"What do you want?" I hissed through gritted teeth, the thumps and rattles of other fights echoing through the house.

So much for the element of surprise. Standard breach formation wasn't doing a lick of good, now was it?

The boy tilted his head to the side, his buddies making the exact same motion with their creepy puppet stares. "Why, I want you, of course."

Yep. Definitely should have kept my mouth shut. Because asking that question made me want to vomit. It reminded me too much of another man. Another man who wanted to use me, possess me.

Well, fuck that.

"No offense, Junior, but I don't want *you*," I growled, my jaw like granite. "So why don't you skedaddle out of my house, hmm? And take your creepy fucking friends with you."

Junior's face crumpled into mock-sadness, complete with a lower lip pout and everything. "That's too bad, Ms. Adler. My master instructed me to bring you to him by any means necessary. And when my master says 'any' he means it." He surveyed me with a dispassionate sort of apathy that only soulless monsters could really pull off. "So, I figure, as long as you're breathing, I don't think he'll care too much."

Cool. Coolcoolcoolcoolcool.

I had a sneaking suspicion who his sire was, and that didn't fill me with any sort of happiness. Because if Junior was older than actual dirt, then his sire could only be Nero.

Super.

Without a great deal of thought—other than how much I wanted to be away from this kid—my power rose in me as fast as a lightning strike. Golden light rocketed from my palms, slamming into Junior and his buddies. And like Aemon had once done with my hands, I wrapped that power around them and sent them all sailing backward.

They knocked into the kitchen table, sending it and the chairs to the floor. The artwork rattled, amazingly still there after Yazzie's tumble through the wall. And all the while, Junior's expression didn't so much as twitch.

Nope. Away just wasn't good enough. I wanted him dead. Dead was better than whatever it was he wanted to do with me.

I had half a mind to squeeze them until they were crushed under the weight of my power, but I knew I just didn't have the juice for something like that. Hell, if the trickle at my nose was any indication, I didn't have the power to do fuck all but pray someone—anyone—would come to save my ass.

I barely took my eyes off the kids to check on Yazzie —who was in human form and very, very unconscious— when a hard hand slammed into me, knocking me into the refrigerator. My power flickered and died as I smacked my head against the metal, my gun sailing out of my hands.

The room went fuzzy, dimming a fair bit. Even sounds were muffled, but that tinkling bell laugh still echoed through my brain at warp speed.

Joy.

I'd always wanted to die in the middle of a horror movie prompt. Really, it was my mission in life, right behind getting dismembered by ghouls or scared to death by ghosts. Why not add in clone doll people as an option?

Gritting my teeth, I forced the world to come back into focus as a rough grip yanked me up by my shoulders. The sickly pale face that would likely be tattooed on my brain for as long as I lived smiled down at me, his red eyes glowing brighter. His mouth curved into a crooked smile, allowing long canines to peek out from the bottom of his lips.

"Oh, you like magic?" he said, his grin spreading just a touch too wide for his face. "I can show you magic."

Bright-red light poured from the hand closest to my face, but whatever it was that he planned on doing to me, it skated right over my skin like water. Frowning, confusion swept over him just long enough for me to sock him right in the solar plexus.

Shock widened his eyes as his magic died, and I hauled my head back and slammed my skull into his, head-butting him square in the nose.

I had a feeling Junior wasn't too versed in his magic not working on someone. Speed he had. Strength, too. But the ability to take a punch?

Not so much.

He let me go, stumbling backward as his nose poured blood, his buddies just standing there like mindless automatons, their noses just as bloody. I scrambled for my gun, taking aim and firing at the first moving body part I found.

A round hit Junior in the shoulder, and he rocked back, his clones copying his motion as blood bloomed on their starched white shirts. Adjusting my aim, I fired again, only this time, it went wide as Junior finally decided bullets hurt and he didn't really care for bleeding.

Dodging the bullet, he leapt over the kitchen island.

He'd barely landed on his feet before red magic bloomed over his arms. Trailing from each finger, the swirls of power flashed across the room, embedding like arrows into the clones' eyes.

And while the thought had crossed my brain that I was about to fight—not *one*, but *five*—ancient *whatever* the fuck they were, no part of said brain had put together the most important bit yet.

Not until that magic hit those clones.

Because until those dead eyes came alive for the first time, I didn't know they *weren't* people. No, they were just extensions of Junior, and if I killed Junior, then it was over. The problem was as soon as that magic hit them, they moved.

And it wasn't like I moved.

No, those clones were just as fast, if not faster than their puppet master, racing for me in the blink of an eye.

I didn't bother aiming for them. *They* were magic, and magic couldn't be killed. No, I locked eyes with Junior and fired, pleased as punch when my bullet hit the side of his neck. I'd have been happier if I'd have hit him in the head, but I was taking what I could get.

But as happy as I was at the blood pouring from his neck, it fizzled out as soon as the wound closed right before my eyes.

Shit. What I wouldn't give for a dagger right about now.

"You know, maybe I tell my master you were killed by the ghouls," he offered, tilting his head to the side, pure malice pouring from his glowing red eyes. "Such a nasty species. Maybe they tore you apart piece by piece." A wicked smile bloomed over his lips. "I'm sure he'll get over it. I'm sure he can find new bait."

As one, the clones pounced, leaving me no option but to attempt an escape from the demolished kitchen. An escape that was swiftly blocked by a wall of red magic.

With nothing else for it, I shot the limited power I had left out of me, allowing it to slam into the clones. I just needed a little bit of space, just a little room to maneuver, and I'd be able to get the fuck out of there.

But the limited rounds left in my gun and small spark remaining in me did little to stop Junior's automatons. With fervor usually reserved for feral animals, they fought the bonds of my magic and seemed unmoved at the bullets landing in their bodies.

Caught in a snare, I shuffled backward, stuck between the red magic that seemed to scald the air around me, and the snapping clones.

Could I have tried to run through that wall of power? Yes.

Did I want to try out the limits of Jimmy's necklace? No, the fuck I did not.

The blissful sound of Yazzie's bear roar filled the room, and I was so glad at having backup that I didn't give so much as a single shit about him dragging me in here in the first place. If we made it out of here, I'd kick his ass later.

Especially, when with a single swipe, he knocked all four clones and one puppet master into the stone island. The red magic fizzled out, and I took that opportunity to run my ass off to the closest cache of weapons. Tearing around the corner, I dodged flying magic and bullets and dove into the dining room.

The China cabinet had been built sometime in the 1700s, the ornate carved feet shaped like a lion's paws. The handles to the glass case were lion heads, their mouths open wide in a roar. Snatching one of those handles, I ripped it wide with so much force, the door broke off its hinges and shattered on the floor.

After this was all over, I'd care that I'd just destroyed a piece of art, but right then, I didn't give that first fuck. I closed my fingers around the hilt of a sword, its blade just longer than a dagger. I'd sharpened that blade not more than three days ago, the edge like a razor. I'd barely had time to turn around before red magic slammed into the cabinet, the impact knocking me into the giant dining room table that no one used.

Junior's creepy smile had turned feral as he sucked in air, his chest a mess of deep gashes and exposed organs. Yazzie's roar echoed through the house, the only assurance I needed that he was still breathing. He'd really done a number on Junior, but those wounds were rapidly healing right before my eyes.

"I'm going to enjoy this," he whispered, his fangs lengthening as he stared at the pulse in my neck. "Your blood will tas—"

Maybe it was his words. Maybe it was because they reminded me too much of another man's voice, another man's threats, but I didn't wait for Junior to finish his little villain monologue. I didn't need to know all the ways he planned on killing me.

Like I should have done to Bishop in that fucking cave, I aimed my blade right for his neck and struck, the sweet pierce of the metal through his flesh a balm to my soul. Shock flooded Junior's expression as blood bloomed from the wound at his neck.

"What was that?" I taunted as he scrabbled at his throat. "I can't hear you."

Then Junior's face lost all expression as his arms hung listlessly at his sides. His whole body wobbled and then his head slid right off his neck, smacking the ground with a satisfying *splat*.

Instantly, his body began to desiccate, crumbling to ash right before my very eyes. I'd have liked to watch him dissolve into nothing, but Yazzie and the others needed my help. I did, however, console myself with stomping my boot right into his disintegrating head.

I had a battle to fight.

16

S carlet magic zoomed past my face as I tried to make my way back to the kitchen to help Yazzie. It didn't matter if I'd killed Junior or not. If the magic under his skin did not, in fact, die with him, Yazzie would be up shit creek without so much as a chopstick for a paddle. Those four clones had enough power all on their lonesome to take the bear down and leaving him stranded didn't sit too well with me.

A part of me wished I'd had the smarts to reload my gun, but with a bloody blade in my hand, I had to admit, I felt prepared enough. Racing through the hall, I dodged bullets and magic alike, barely managing to get back to the kitchen unscathed. Weapons drawn and ready, I nearly took Yazzie's head off when he bounded through the half-demolished kitchen entry, clouds of ash sticking to his fur.

Chuffing at me, he kept going, and like I'd been doing all fucking day, I followed him. What else was I going to do? Ducking under blistering spells, I trailed after the giant bear as he busted through the house to the parlor. His roar rattled my ears, making the whole room freeze for a second. A moment later, Yazzie's mouth latched onto the shoulder of another blond, this one older looking, if not as long in the tooth as Junior, taller, and with far less polish.

But he didn't yelp when Yazzie munched on his shoulder. Instead, magic skated over his hands as he yanked the bear's teeth right out of his flesh, the crack of Yazzie's jaw making me sick. Yazzie slumped to the ground—unconscious, not dead—but my relief was short-lived.

This wasn't a man.

This was a clone.

And as much as I wanted to help, fighting this copy wasn't going to do a lick of good. Björn rushed the clone, knocking him away from Yazzie as his own magic lit his hands. A sonic boom of power hit the ground right in front of the clone before a flash fire consumed him.

Unable to stay and watch, I spun on a heel and raced

upstairs toward the loudest of the battle. Thomas sailed over the railing backward, nearly taking me out on the steps as he landed. The best I could do was send out that little bit of power I had to try and cushion the fall. Still, he landed hard, his bloody body crumpling to the floor.

But as old as Thomas was, no way in hell would a little fall keep him down.

Any second now...

Grumbling, I rushed to the landing and hauled him up. He was a fuck of a lot heavier than I remembered. "Jesus, fuck, did you swallow lead?"

He groaned, and I fought off the urge to elbow him in the gut. Then again, said gut was a crisscrossed mishmash of healing cuts and *not*-so-healed cuts that had to have been far deeper than I ever wanted to think about.

"Get off your ass, vampire," I hissed, dragging him with me as I scaled back up the stairs. The steps were far harder than I wanted them to be with his dead weight.

"Wha?" he grumbled, struggling to find his feet.

Jesus, Mary, and all the saints. What the hell had those fucks done to him? It was one thing to be at the entrance to the Underworld. It was quite another to get your ass handed to you by a bunch of *whatever* the hell they were. Thomas was an ancient. Even then, his power practically poured off him in waves.

If Junior was old, Thomas could have passed as his grandpa. So, what the hell had tapped him out so bad that I was dragging his sorry ass back up the stairs? Something told me I didn't want to know.

Then I really let my elbow fly, figuring pain was just about the only thing that would wake his ass up. An indignant "Oof" and loss of his weight had my lips tipping up—even though I was ready to shit a litter of kittens. I didn't like Thomas—probably never would—but him getting back in this fight with me was a far sight better than doing it without him.

"Gods, you're worse than Sloane. At least she isn't sadistic." He removed his arm from my shoulder, crouching on his knees behind the cover of a display cabinet. "Got a magic spell in your back pocket that'll help, or are we winging this bullshit?"

Sloane spent a year of her life rampaging through the city streets of Ascension, had a body count I couldn't even fathom, and I was the sadistic one?

"Aww. Did I give you a boo-boo?" I taunted, passing over my gun. "Does this count as a magic spell?"

Thomas checked the chamber and shrugged. "It'll do."

"Tell me," I whispered, trying to gauge the lay of the

land, "do all of them look alike, or are they different people?"

Thomas' gaze seemed to laser-lock on the side of my face. "Alike. Why?"

"The one I killed downstairs could clone himself. But when I took his head, they all died. If we can find the real one—"

"*Fuck*," Thomas hissed, cutting off my musings. "Was he short, Slavic accent, kinda sickly-looking?"

"You knew him?" And yes, I used the past tense because that motherfucker was *dead*.

Thomas nodded, checking the chamber of the Glock again as he ground his teeth. "Nero's *children*," he spat, curling his lip as if the word tasted bad. "That was probably Johan. And if Johan is dead, then the fucker terrorizing us now is Lars. Nero turned them to punish Ingrid."

Bright light poured from my hands as second-hand rage and shame filled me. Nero had turned Ingrid against her will when she was eight years old. I knew very little about how turnings worked two thousand years ago, but today turning a child was forbidden. It labeled him as the worst sort of predator and made me sick to my stomach.

How after all he'd done, could he turn someone else to punish her? "What the fuck does that mean?"

Instead of answering me, Thomas stood, crept out of our hiding spot, and took three shots. Without any answers, I followed, ready to lay waste to any of those bastards still standing. A copy of the kid from downstairs stood in between Tobin's computer lair and my bedroom, the door to which was filled with a sweating and rage-filled Jimmy brandishing his sword.

In the space behind Jimmy was Dahlia and Jay working on a scarily still Tobin. Dahlia was shoving awfully familiar blue tonics down his throat while Jay compressed his chest.

Oh. Oh, no.

But Tobin's soul wasn't calling for me and I didn't see Sloane anywhere, so I had to hope for the best.

Lars' crimson magic collided with Jimmy's gold, making flaming orange sparks as they exploded midair, knocking them both backward. Taking the small glimmer of an opportunity we had, I shot what was left of my power right at the bastard, shoving him over the railing, just as he'd done with Thomas.

Just before he hit the ground, Björn's odd magic slammed into him, powering whatever he was onto the floor. The wood splintered upon impact, but no matter how much magic held him down, Lars still stood, fighting against our bonds.

But instead of firing back, he retreated, racing from

the magic itself. He powered through the parlor and crashed through the front window, escaping into the neighborhood.

"I'm following him. Bas, you coming?" Bjorn called up the stairs before trailing after Lars through the now-broken window.

Jay switched with Bastian on compressions before the big man jumped over the railing to follow, the stairs evidently too much work.

And then it was quiet—only Dahlia's murmurings, Jay's compressions, and Jimmy's heavy breathing. No more gunshots. No more red magic.

But Tobin was fading, and fast.

With nothing else for it, I called that awful dark soul. Johan's soul, the only ghost I could call to me with those fucking wards on my house. As soon as he arrived, he coated my skin like slime, his darkness making me want to puke. I tried not to see the horrors of his soul, but two thousand years of horror was too much for me to block out.

Stumbling, I blindly headed in the direction of a bathroom, praying I found a toilet before the meager contents of my stomach came up. I barely made it, losing my lunch as Johan's life flashed before my eyes.

Or what parts of it I could actually see. Like the ghouls, sections of Johan's life were blank, either by his own hand or from Nero's doing. And Nero featured heavily in his memories. I thought I knew what it meant to be turned as a child. I thought I knew how deplorable it was.

I didn't know the half of it.

When my stomach finally gave up the ghost, I stumbled back to Tobin, offering the immense power to him, offloading the rest to Yazzie downstairs, who was still unconscious. No matter how much juice a two-thousand-year-old soul had, I didn't want any part of Johan anywhere near me.

Giving as much as I could, I observed with wonder as Johan's dark power finally did something good. Cuts sealed, blood dried, and the hollow, waxy appearance to Tobin's skin melted away. I felt the instant Yazzie woke, his shifter healing doing the rest of the work for me.

Tobin coughed, taking in fresh air for the first time since I didn't know when. His lids cracked, showing me his honey-brown irises.

"I'm sorry," he croaked, trying to sit up. "I'm so sorry."

Jay, Dahlia, and I put a hand on him, trying to keep him down.

"Lay still," Dahlia insisted, fishing a blue vial from the pouch at her hip. "You need more healing."

I remembered vividly just how awful those tonics

tasted and didn't envy Tobin one bit. "You didn't do anything wrong. You warned us good, kiddo. We knew what we were walking into."

That was a bold-faced lie, but Tobin didn't need to know that. But there was no way to know what was in store for us here. Not with Sarina out of commission and this place warded out the wazoo.

"Anyone have enough juice to get those tainted wards off this house?" I asked, helping Tobin up and onto my bedside chair. He was bloody and weak but breathing.

"Yeah, I can. I'll tell Hildy everyone's alive," Jimmy muttered before pressing a kiss to Jay's temple. "That is if he's still out there."

Hildy was supposed to follow any stragglers, but a part of me hoped he hadn't. I didn't want Hildy anywhere near Nero's children. No way no how.

Jay stood, and I wrapped him up in a hug. I didn't like my friends in danger—didn't want this for any of them. Especially Jay.

"You good?" I croaked, still shaken from Johan's soul and glad that Jay was still with me.

He returned my embrace, easing my nerves just a bit. "Yeah. Not a scratch, D. Not even a snack attack, either."

"Is that what we're calling going feral these days?"

Thomas drawled, his snide comment fair, if unwarranted, especially given our history.

Pushing back from Jay, I stood in between the two vamps ready to lay Thomas out... just as soon as I absorbed another ghost or five. "Says the man who went feral like a week ago and nearly took my head off, but whatever."

Thomas' expression went abashed for a single solitary second before the cool apathetic mask was back. "Yes, well..."

"*Yes, well,*" I parroted, mocking his aloof tone.

"Aldy?" Yazzie yelled, bounding up the staircase in his—thankfully—human form. Intact and fully healed, I sort of envied the accelerated healing of shifters in general.

He slid to a stop in front of Tobin and yanked him right out of the chair into a bear hug.

Yes. The pun was intended.

Tobin flopped like a fish in Yazzie's arms as the giant shifter hugged him close.

"I thought I told you to engage the security system while you were alone in the house. We set that up together, you idiot," Yazzie scolded, setting the smaller man down and ruffling his hair like a big brother would.

Tobin ducked his head. "I forgot."

"We all fuck up sometimes," I offered, trying to keep

my cool. I had asked Tobin to research about eight zillion things for me in the last twenty-four hours. I couldn't blame him for this.

"Yeah," Thomas piped in. "Kind of like busting through the fucking house like the *Kool-Aid Man* blowing the entire element of surprise. Is the back door even on its hinges anymore?"

Chuckling, I pulled away from the group. No, the back door was not on its hinges, and yes, that would need to be fixed before my eye started to twitch. But right then, I needed to do a sweep, making sure no one else was left in this house that wasn't supposed to be here.

Typically, I did this with a loaded gun, Hildy, and enough suspense to wear my molars to nubs. Now? I was just so relieved that Tobin was okay, and no one died, that I was far laxer than I should have been. So, when I trundled down to the basement, it wasn't with the same vigilance as I usually had.

The first thing that made me realize I was chucked back into the "fucked" column? Tripping over a very warm, very still body. In the dim light of the basement, it took me a second to recognize the absolute hamburger that was Acker's face. A single open eye—since the other one was swelled shut—found *my* face, horror stamped all over it. He tried to speak, but nothing came out.

The second? A chilling voice I'd only ever heard in the memories of the dead.

"Ah, Ms. Adler. I see you're still on the loose," he said, sending a chill down my spine as I slowly turned to face him. His expression was placid, jovial even, with a smooth brow and an unbothered smile. "And it just goes to show, if you want something done right, you must do it yourself."

The vampire known only as Nero smiled, showing no hint of the fangs he kept at bay. And I was so focused on his face, that I never saw the fist aimed right for my temple.

17

The copper taste of pennies in my mouth registered first. That, and the fact that I was hanging by my wrists. Shoulders screaming, I cracked my eyelids as consciousness finally found me. Silver manacles with dark-black sigils etched in the cuffs cut into my wrists. Attached to a long chain that hung over a wicked hook in the stone ceiling, my bonds didn't look like they were breaking anytime soon.

I wasn't bleeding yet, but if I hung much longer, I would.

Perfect. Just perfect.

Now I had a conundrum here. I could either pretend to still be unconscious and assess the situation before attempting my escape, or I could try the limits of my powers and yank that hook out of the wall with my bare hands. But that was if I had enough power to do anything more than just breathe.

"Darby?" a familiar voice croaked, and I abandoned the faking school of thought immediately.

Eyes popping wide and feet finding their place, I swiveled to find Shiloh in a similar situation as me, hanging from a hook in the middle of what had to be a dungeon. "Shi?"

The witch was in her original form, her dark hair hanging down her face in bloody mats. She'd only been gone for a few hours, right? But her fingers were blue with blood loss and her face was a bruised mess.

How long had I been out?

"What happened to you?" It had taken less than an hour to figure out Shiloh and Acker were missing. Less than an hour to realize that the ghoul attack had either been a distraction or coordinated assault.

Less than an hour to become well and truly fucked.

Shiloh gave me a halfhearted smile. "Ghouls attacked us on the road to Ingrid's. But they had a *thing* with them. He wasn't a vampire and wasn't a mage but a mix of both. And he could multiply." Tears filled her eyes, and she shook her head. "I tried everything, but I failed. I came here to help—to make sure you didn't do this alone—and now look at us."

I had to wonder if I'd asked her to stay with us, if I'd

insisted on all of us sticking together if she would have gotten taken. I also had to wonder if I hadn't gone off half-cocked to check the stupid security system Tobin had forgotten to set if I would be in the same damn predicament.

"The ghouls attacked us, too. And Ingrid's. And the Warden house. Though, it wasn't ghouls at the Warden house. It was two of those creepy hybrid things."

I didn't want to admit out loud that I'd been the one to kill one of Nero's children. I had a feeling I was in enough trouble as it was.

Hildy. If you can hear me, I'm in trouble. Please.

Hell, I was half-tempted to call Aemon himself. What had he said? Just say his name aloud three times, right? Yeah, I was about to *Beetlejuice* this bitch.

But if I called him—if I summoned that fucking demon for real—then I had no doubt I'd owe him. Before, he had always come on his own, doing what he thought would get in my good graces. If I called him?

Well, that was a price I didn't know if I would be willing to pay.

"There are others here," Shiloh whispered, her gaze flitting toward the dark corner of the mostly empty room. "I can hear them."

I tried to focus on whatever it was that she was hearing, but all that filled my ears was my own breath sawing in and out of my lungs and the frightened tripping of my heart. Flitting my gaze about, I attempted to catalogue where we were, but all I found was a chalkboard filled with sacred geometry, and a single pillar candle half-burnt out on a barrel of who knew what.

Not promising.

Twisting the chains, I pivoted on my tiptoes, trying to assess just how screwed we were. I'd originally thought we were in a dungeon, but dungeons didn't typically have windows. An old-fashioned lead glass window stood tucked away in the corner of the dark room, the minimal light from the waning moon casting odd shadows through the warped diamond pattern on the rough wood floor.

On the same wall as the window was a messy, dusty desk filled with aged parchment and more candles, their burnt-out carcasses pooling on the paper. Had I stepped back in time when Nero knocked me out? Would I find a quill and ink pot next?

"Where are we?" I asked, confusion reigning supreme in my brain. "And why did you leave? What were you going to ask Astrid?"

I seriously doubted Shiloh would have been able to get anything out of the council's resident witch bitch, but the mystery of it all was nagging at me.

Shiloh huffed a dispirited little laugh. "I have no fucking clue where we are. Wherever it is, I seriously doubt we're in Knoxville."

I hated to think Shiloh was right, but I feared with each passing second, she was. Sure, there were places in the city I'd had yet to see, but I doubted "old country root cellar" was a popular design choice.

"And Astrid?" she continued, her tone turning bitter as her lip curled in disgust. "I wanted her to confirm what I already knew. Something that doesn't mean a fucking thing now that I'm here."

Rolling my eyes, I let my impatience get the better of me. "Share with the class, Shi. After all, I *am* just hanging here."

With the side of her arm, Shiloh attempted—and failed—to shove her hair behind an ear. "The witch I saw? Candace? She was supposedly dead for twenty years before she showed up in that park, right? Well, I had a hunch *all* the dead witches found over the last week were like that."

Her brain was making more leaps than mine was because I didn't understand anything that had just come out of her mouth. "Explain."

Shiloh groaned, shifting from one foot to the other. "Candy was said to have killed herself, but no one ever found a body. Maybe she didn't take her own life. Maybe she was like me, wearing someone else's face. If that was the case, then maybe *all* those other witches were, too."

Which would explain why she'd needed Astrid. Astrid would know about any witches brought to justice or major deaths in the community. "And that's why the witches that were going missing weren't the ones turning up dead," I murmured, the pieces coming together. "Because when they die—"

"Their glamour dies with them." Shiloh nodded, finishing my sentence.

But it couldn't be all of them, right?

"You don't think all the missing witches are in the arcane version of WITSEC, do you?" I'd heard of a few people entering into the Federal Witness Security Program in my days on the force, but I had no idea if the arcane world had their own version of it. Somehow—especially in this day and age—I figured the concept of hiding was slowly going away.

Though, unlike humans, arcaners could change their whole fucking face.

"Nope. Just the dead ones, I think. Which doesn't bode well for someone who's faked her own death. Namely me."

Yeah, I'd already put that together, but still, none of it made much sense. What was the goal, other than draining the ley lines? It wasn't like you could just stuff the power away for a rainy day, it had to be used for *something*.

I just didn't know what it was.

"This is going to sound callous as fuck, but... What does he get out of killing you? I've seen the files on Nero. For better or worse, the death he brings usually has a purpose. Granted, it's usually a fucked-up, awful purpose, but a purpose, nonetheless. Why kill witches with other faces?"

Did it nearly make me gag saying one even remotely positive thing about the man who was solidly classified as a mass-murdering, child-stealing, blight on the world? Yes.

Was I still having trouble not puking? Also, yes.

"I have a theory, and you're not going to like it," she announced, standing up on her tiptoes as she tried to give herself a little slack.

When had I ever liked a theory that involved murder?

Never. The answer was never.

Groaning, I also got on my tiptoes, the biting ache too much for me to think clearly. I needed to give my wrists some relief, or when the time came to defend myself, I'd be as useless as a newborn baby colt.

"I'm all ears," I said on a sigh, the faint trickle of relief tempered by the ache in my feet.

"Candace had a special ability on top of her witch

powers. Not every witch has that. Not all of us can tap into the gifts our ancestors have bestowed on us. Candy could bend light, make herself or even whole buildings invisible. Cloaking magic, illusion magic—she could do it all. That's why they suspected her of stealing. All the best light benders have been thieves of one form or another."

I had a bad feeling about whatever she was going to say next.

"And you think he, what? Stole that from her?" I was spitballing, but what the fuck else was I going to do? Getting out of these chains wasn't going to be easy.

Shiloh nodded. "There wasn't another reason to kill her. Not that I can see. But you can't just take a witch's gifted power. She has to will it to you. They can't be stolen—not even by a syphon. That kind of power? It has to be given."

"So he tortured her until she gave it up. Or he tranced her. Or he threatened someone she loved." And all of that was just super, but what did he get out of taking Shiloh? "And you? You got some wacky power under your belt you haven't told me about?"

Shiloh's gaze left me then, and she studied the hook above her head. "Yep. Which is real unfortunate, considering the only person still alive that knows about it besides me? Is Astrid."

That caught my attention. "Witch Bitch Astrid knows shit about you I don't know?"

"Unfortunately. She was Prudence's best friend. Astrid and Prue and my mother helped me bind it. Helped me keep it hidden."

Rage ignited in my belly. Prudence Whiteshaw was dead, killed by young upstart coven members ready to branch out on their own. Shiloh's mother was also gone, lost to a spell gone wrong. All that was left was Shiloh and Astrid.

Man, I knew that bitch had to be up to something.

"So she's in on this shit? Helping him?" Leading her own people to slaughter? It reminded me so much of Mariana, I wanted to scream.

"Maybe. Maybe she talked. Maybe she offered information, not knowing it put me in danger. Mayb—"

"Maybe she's a self-serving narcissist with half a fucking brain cell and zero self-preservation instincts?" I really shouldn't have pulled that punch yesterday. Was it yesterday? Maybe it was the day before. I should have caved in her stupid, lying, cheating skull and have been done with it.

Sure, I'd probably be cooling my heels in a jail cell, but was that so bad considering where I was? I'd take human jail over this shit any day.

"So what is it, this power he wants so much? And

206 | ANNIE ANDERSON

what does it have to do with the ley lines?" The time for secrecy and games was over. We needed info and a way out, and we needed it now.

Shiloh didn't look at me. Instead, she closed her eyes and gritted her teeth. A dark sort of light unraveled from her chest, spilling from her body as it coated her skin. It veined up her neck in broken branches of darkness, crawling up her jaw as it hit her eyes. Shiloh's eyes opened, the brown irises gone.

All that was left was blackness. No pupil. No sclera. No life.

Just a cold blackness, the likes of which I'd never seen from my friend.

Shiloh gripped her chain and jumped, catching the links as her feet dangled in the air. Then fist over fist, she hauled herself up to the hook in the ceiling. How she did this with blue hands and beat to shit, I didn't know, but I had a feeling whatever power that hit her might have something to do with it.

She reached the hook and used it as a handhold while she flicked the chain off the open end. A moment later she was back on the rough floor, dragging her chains behind her as she came to me.

While it was super awesome that my friend got free from that stupid hook, the look on her face did not spell good things for me. "Shiloh?"

Maybe it was my recent run-in with Bishop. Maybe I just didn't think I could do another betrayal, but I really wanted my friend to still be in there somewhere.

"Why do you smell like chaos, Darby? Like smoke and blood and death? Like strife?" Shiloh asked, her murmur chilling me to the bone.

A nervous chuckle escaped my lips. "Just lucky, I guess?"

Shiloh shook her head, the slow, calculated movement doing nothing to ease my nerves. "Not luck. The hand dealt to you by Fate. Your father was Death, your mother chaos. And the two mixed together brought us you. A St. James heir without the St. James name. That makes us cousins, you know. Dahlia, too. And Poppy. There are more of us than you know. More family than you could shake a stick at."

I vaguely remembered Mariana boasting about her own mother being a St. James witch. It was how she'd been able to oust Shiloh and take over the whole of the Knoxville coven.

"That's great, Shi," I cooed, trying to placate whatever it was that had Shiloh looking like she wanted to take a chunk out of me. "But I'm not a witch, remember?"

She tilted her head to the side, a soft, floaty smile

crossing her lips. "No, you're not. That makes it better, I think."

Made *what* better?

Then she was just gone. One second Shiloh was far too close to me for comfort, and the next, Lars was standing in her place. The crash of Shiloh hitting the stone wall reverberated through the room, but I couldn't take my eyes off the hybrid in front of me. Disheveled and rage-filled, his red eyes locked on mine.

"You killed my brother, you bitch. Now you're going to pay."

18

L ars' hand latched onto my neck, squeezing the breath right out of me. It didn't matter that I was taller than the vamp hybrid. Didn't matter who my parents were, or what training I'd had. I was still cuffed and chained and practically helpless.

As someone who prided herself on never *being* helpless, it was a tough pill to swallow. That was, if I *could* swallow.

Spots danced in front of my eyes as Lars squeezed, my legs kicking listlessly at his shins as the weight of my body yanked at the cuffs. The metal bit into my skin, but I barely felt it. Not with Lars' cold, clammy touch at my throat.

"I'm going to watch you choke," he hissed, his face so close to mine that I could feel his breath on my skin.

"Over and over again. And then I'm going to rip every inch of skin from your bones. I'm go—"

Lars' eyes widened as his words cut off, his grip going slack. Oxygen flooded my lungs, and I was so busy coughing that I almost missed the trickle of blood that snaked from the corner of his mouth as his hand fell away completely. He stumbled backward, his skin graying out as it cracked with age, desiccating right before my very eyes.

Then his body dissolved, crumbling to ash as a placid Nero dropped the heart in his hand and licked his bloody fingers clean. If I saw him on the street and didn't know who he was, I'd likely think he was attractive. Over six feet and lean, he had pretty gray eyes set in a chiseled tan face. He wore his medium-brown hair longish, sweeping in gentle waves to his chin.

Like I said, he was pretty.

Pretty fucking crazy.

"I told you to wait, didn't I? Told you she was important. You should have listened to me," the ancient vampire groused, staring at the ashes on his shoe with disgust. He lifted his foot, shaking off the dust before locking his gaze on me, that blank expression making me wish I was somewhere—anywhere—but there. "Look what you made me do," Nero accused, clucking his tongue at me as he shook his head.

Sure. Because I totally made that stupid kid wrap his hand around my own throat and damn near strangle me to death. I wanted to say *all* that out loud, but if there was anyone likely to rip out my tongue for sass, it was Nero.

Plus, I was too busy sucking in oxygen to say much of anything at all.

"Lars has been with me for two millennia, Ms. Adler. And here you come along and take two of my best warriors from me in a single day." Nero surveyed me in a way that had my skin crawling. "Lars and Johan. Gone," he barked, snapping his fingers. "Just like that. I don't know if I'm impressed or enraged."

His eyes lit at the word, a red film slowly falling over his irises like a heavy blanket. Enraged then.

Super.

"I tend to have that effect on people. Don't sweat it. I'm sure you have plenty of minions running around here somewhere."

Did I actually say that out loud? Yep.

Was it the dumbest shit I have ever said? Also, yes.

Did I regret it? Well, the jury was still out on that one.

If I was going out—and I had a sneaking suspicion I was, considering I was chained to a hook in the ceiling while an ancient sadist contemplated me like a side of beef—then I was going to tell this murdering, pedophilic monster just what I thought of him. It was better than dying quiet, that was for sure.

Maybe if I pissed him off, he'd make it quick.

Nero's smile was like something out of a nightmare. "They told me you were a flippant little thing. I'm so glad the rumors are true. It'll make this so much sweeter when I break you."

Snorting, I shook my head. "Is that the best you can do? As old as you are, I kind of figured you'd be…" I paused, studying him with the same dispassionate stare he'd given me. "Scarier. The files made you seem like the boogeyman. Pity."

His face hardened to granite, his jaw clenching in affront. "You will regret not holding your tongue when I rip it out of your head."

A giggle bubbled up my throat. "Sure thing, babe. I totally believe you. Even though you just killed a guy you've been with for two thousand years because he was going to kill me." I clucked my tongue at him, parroting the simpering tone he had just given me. "You and I both know you aren't doing shit. You need me for something. Don't you?"

Okay, so ninety percent of that was bravado, but really, it was all I had at this point.

Hildenbrand O'Shea. Anytime you want to come get me, that would be great.

Nero stepped forward, his movement too fast for me to actually see. Just like Shiloh had done only moments ago, one second, he was several paces away and the next, he was in my face. Fitting a single finger under my chin, he yanked up my jaw so I was staring right in his eyes.

"They said you were smart, though I doubt you've put it all together. Yes, I do need something from you, and I'll get it, too. Have you figured out what it is yet?"

I decided humoring him was the best course of action. "Let's see. You're taking witches with other faces —witches with special abilities. Probably tucking those away for a rainy day. You're draining ley lines. Amassing power. Now, as someone whose soul is on the chopping block and a demon out looking for you, I can only guess it has something to do with that. Tell me—am I getting warm?"

Though, what this had to do with me, I hadn't a clue. I didn't have a power I could will away. Especially not to him.

He studied me, his scarlet eyes zeroing in on my neck. "Lukewarm at best. And here I thought you were a good detective. I guess without any ghosts in your ear, you're not so smart, are you?"

He knew Hildy wasn't here. He knew it because he'd made it so. I guessed that's why Hildy wasn't answering my call. It just figured that wherever I was, was warded just like my house had been.

Rude.

"Aww. You hurt my feelings," I mocked sarcastically. "Okay, Mr. Wizard. Enlighten me, then. What is your dastardly plan? You going to take over the world? Shocking. *So* original."

Actually, with enough ley line juice, he could do a lot of damage. Maybe more than a lot.

Nero's smile curved into a certified grin—a grin that seemed boyish and malevolent all at the same time. "It took me a long time to come up with this plan. So many hiccups along the way. So many grave talkers sticking their noses where they didn't belong. You know if your grandfather hadn't been so nosy, he'd probably still be alive today. Tell me—how *is* Hildenbrand?"

So that was one question answered. I mean, how many other ancient vampires were just draining ley lines via poltergeists all willy-nilly like? My guess? Zero. "Peachy. Living the dream."

And considering he had an entire ley line's worth of power in his ghost form, lost none of his powers, and could turn corporeal whenever he wanted, I probably wasn't lying.

"You know, had he not stolen all that energy, I wouldn't have known my plan was possible. Too bad you won't be able to thank him for me. But it's so much more than just collecting the power, isn't it? I don't want to just hoard it. I want to be it. Pure, unadulterated power. Do you know what kind of being that is?"

Okay, he'd lost me.

Unbidden by my frown, he squished my face with a single hand. "Can't you figure it out? Enough ley line power, enough abilities, and I won't have to worry about some puny prince pissed off that he got outsmarted. I'll be a god. Unfortunately," he mused, showing me the back of his hand, the skin decayed with bright-red weeping sores spanning the flesh from knuckle to wrist, "this vessel isn't up to the task. As much as it has served me over the years, I'll need something a little more... *sturdy*. And what better body to pick than the one who gave me my first dose of power?"

Nero tucked his finger under my chin again, only this time the sharp bite of a talon sliced into my flesh. "Call your boyfriend for me, sweetheart."

What had Johan said about bait? Oh, that's right. Me. I was the bait.

Shit.

"I don't have a boyfriend. But if you mean Deimos' son, you summoned him once, didn't you? To make your deal? You can call him yourself."

His talon pressed further into my flesh, making me

hiss. "See, I would, but I need him off guard. Worried even. If *I* call him, then he'll come in guns blazing, ready to reap my soul—dead or not. But if *you* call him, then I get what I want. It's simple really. Even you should be able to figure it out."

I wasn't going to say his name. I wasn't even going to think it. Not because I cared for him. Not because I wanted him safe. Not because he'd saved my life one too many times.

And certainly not because he'd fixed my fucking chair.

My refusal was more so the deranged vampire with a literal god complex didn't actually become a god.

"Sorry. Maybe I'm too stupid to understand. Or maybe I'm too sane. Either way? You can fuck off."

Nero's smile grew wide, revealing fangs that should *not* be able to fit inside that mouth. They weren't needlelike or sharp canines, but both. Long sharklike incisors snapped right in front of my face.

"I was hoping you'd say that."

Hildy? Sloane? I know you guys have to be busy but—

The ancient vampire flashed his talons in my face, the wickedly sharp nails far longer than I'd like— especially since they were mere inches from my cheek. Ever so slowly, he reached for my skin, pressing the nail into the tender flesh beside my eye. The edge was so sharp, I barely felt it at first, the bite only coming after he raked it down my jaw.

A hiss escaped my lips, but I quickly reined it in, schooling my features to a bland mask.

He tilted his head to the side, glee tinting his expression. "Such spirit. I wonder how long it will take to break you."

Clenching my jaw, warmth oozed from the wound and raced down my neck. The scent beckoned Nero, his irises almost burgundy with his hunger. But he didn't drink from me. No, that would be too easy. Instead, he traced those talons through the blood, making shallow, stinging cuts all the way down my neck.

The fucker was just playing with me at this point.

Then he flashed those talons again, only this time, he slashed them across my middle. Cutting through my shirt, my body armor, those sharp nails dug into my skin. Ripping. Tearing. There was nothing I could do but scream, the agony flooding every single pain center I had.

But he was far from done.

Nero had eons to perfect his torture techniques, and he utilized each of them one by one, giving me a master class on pain. From my stomach, he moved methodically to my knees, severing the ligament behind my right knee and then my left. My legs refused to hold me as I howled, the torment just beginning.

"This can all be over, you know," he whispered in my ear, his hot breath on my skin making me wish I would just pass out. Hell, I'd pray for unconsciousness at this point. "Just say his name."

Nero's pitch was nothing if not calm, the fake soothing tone making me do the only thing I could. As soon as he pulled away from my ear, I spat right in his face. Saliva ran down his cheek, and that was about the last satisfying thing I felt for a long time.

He wiped at his face, smearing my spit and blood. A second later he backhanded me, the strike twisting me round and round on that stupid fucking hook, the blistering heat of the impact both rocking my head on my neck and waking me up.

I only had to last. I could do that. I could keep my mouth shut.

Stopping my spin, Nero latched onto my hair, yanking my head back so I was forced to look him right in the eye. "Say. His. Name."

"No," I croaked. "Never."

He dug his talons into the tender flesh at the back of my arms. "Say it."

All I could do was scream, unable to hold in the bitter agony.

This went on for hours. The sound of Nero's sadistic laughter echoed in my ears with each new cut or broken bone, each new tear to my skin, each new torture. And every time I screamed, he would tell me to call out for Aemon.

Eventually, darkness came for me, the blessed bliss of unconsciousness, but it never lasted.

The water came next—ice-cold sheets of it poured over me, stealing every last bit of my relief. Gasping for breath, I fought for air, sucking in oxygen as soon as the water stopped. I was no longer hanging from a hook. No, I had been strapped to a giant metal "X," my wrists and ankles bound in steel cuffs.

I was on a large stage, but I wasn't alone. Across from me was a still-sleeping Shiloh, her head hanging listlessly, just as the first witch's had been. Bloody matted hair hung in clumps, obscuring her face, but I knew it was her.

"Oh, good. You're awake." Nero's deranged smile was tempered by the open, weeping sore on his cheek. "Just in time for the festivities."

A line of red-robed children swept through the room. Each one blonde. Each one no older than Ingrid had been when she was turned. One by one they took their seats, whispering excitedly to each other like real school children would. Then, at the very end of the line, walked in a tall man I knew all too well.

It made sense that he was here. A nightmare come to life.

Bishop.

19

In the back of my mind, I knew he would be involved somehow. Like the shadow in the corner of your eye, he was always there, lurking, ready to strike when I least expected it. Bishop La Roux was nothing like the man I believed him to be. A year ago, I imagined him to be a mysterious mage sent to help me. Thought he was a knight—or maybe a rogue—with a good heart, if questionable morals, and a compass that always pointed north.

And like he'd done to so many others, he fooled me.

With spells.

With lies.

With his attention.

Wrapping his fake persona up in a bow, he'd pulled

the wool over my eyes, disguising obsession as love, and control as caring. He'd taken my will away.

So yes, it made sense for him to be here. With Essex dead and his deeds exposed, he'd need a new master to hide behind. It just figured that Bishop would pick the worst of the bunch. He'd worked with Essex and Mariana, knowing exactly who they were and what they stood for—following implicitly under the umbrella of survival.

Why *wouldn't* he follow Nero?

And that fear I should have felt at seeing him? It was gone.

Maybe it was the heavy blood loss. Could be the hours and hours of torture. Or maybe it was that death was so close. I could feel it breathing down my neck as my skin prickled from the cold and the numbness settled into my limbs.

Hurting was good. Hurting meant I was alive. Hurting kept me awake.

But the pain had faded to the background, making my eyelids droop and my breathing slow.

As soon as Bishop's gaze fell on me, he stopped following those children and darted right in my direction, a swirl of black magic coalescing in his palm. Vaguely, I still felt the necklace at my throat, protecting me from magical harm, but just like I'd found out with the zombies, that didn't mean anything. If Bishop wanted me dead, he'd figure out a way to get the job done.

One way or another.

Before he could reach me, Nero stepped solidly in his path. The ancient vampire let loose a slap, knocking into Bishop so hard he flew off his feet, landing in a heap on the rough wood floor.

"We've discussed your payment, haven't we?" Nero simpered, picking Bishop up off the floor by the collar of his shirt. "You do your job, she gives me what I need, and *then* you can have her. I won't have you spoiling her before I can get my prize, mage."

Bishop's face twisted, an expression I'd only witnessed firsthand in the caves. He'd backstab Nero the first chance he got—I was sure of it. Funny, that sounded like a whole fuck load of "not my problem." The vamp would figure out just how treacherous Bishop could be soon enough.

I was sort of hoping they'd eat each other or something.

"Fine," Bishop hissed, ripping his shirt out of Nero's fist. "But if you think she'll break with torture, you've picked the wrong girl. Darby Adler is a martyr through and through. If she thought it was the right thing, she'd sit there and suffer until you cut her head off. You want help with your little…" He trailed off as his gaze fell on the weeping sores on Nero's hand. *"Problem?* You might want my advice on breaking her."

Oh, fuck you, you pedantic prick.

Nero's lip curled as he surveyed the mage. "Just do what you're told. You have a problem with that?"

Bishop didn't deign to answer him, and simply strode across the stage to Shiloh. Fisting his hand in her hair, he hauled her head up and slapped her still-unconscious face. What had Lars done to her? What had Nero?

And what did they plan to do?

Nero wanted power, power, and more power. Shiloh had it. She had more than I'd ever thought she did—so much it scared me. And if Nero added to what was clearly trying to escape his flesh, he'd let Bishop hurt me. He'd let him do whatever the mage wanted if it meant he got what he needed.

His vessel.

I contemplated calling for the prince, not wanting to even think his name for fear he'd come. I knew the necklace made it so he couldn't hear my thoughts, but I'd always suspected he had another way to find me. Maybe by the way he'd locked himself out of my head.

If he ever really did.

"Rise and shine, witch," Bishop spat, pinching Shiloh's cheeks in his hand.

Slowly, Shiloh roused, her eyelids fluttering as consciousness finally found her. A part of me wished she'd have stayed out, the faint tendril of pain filtering into my brain. If my fate was also hers, I'd prefer we all avoid the torture.

"Wakey, wakey. We've got a schedule to keep," Bishop muttered, grabbing her pinky finger and snapping the bone.

Shiloh's eyes popped wide as she screamed, the pained cry hurting me far more than my own torture had. Tears pooled in her brown eyes as she whimpered, but she didn't say a word. I hated to say that the lack of her former all-black gaze had me mighty uneasy as I stood strapped to the wood, the likelihood of us getting out of this dwindling by the second.

"Oh, good," Nero crowed, clapping his hands as if Bishop torturing her was the height of entertainment. "I'm so glad you decided to join us, Ms. St. James. I've met some of your former coven members. They have been most helpful."

He sauntered closer, a lustful gleam to his eyes. "Tell me—do you think you can help me, too?"

For the second time in a single day, another woman spat in Nero's face. Shiloh's saliva was stained red with blood, and just like he'd done with me, the backhand came out of nowhere, rocking her head to the side.

"So feisty, aren't you? So much power in those veins. I can smell it in your blood." Nero closed the distance, pressing his chest against hers as he sniffed her neck. Then he snaked out his sore-infested tongue, licking her cheek before stepping away. "All that juicy chaos just filling you up. Can't you feel it?"

Her eyes narrowed as her lip curled. "Fuck you."

"All in due time," Nero quipped, his grin wide and filled with those repulsive shark teeth. "But first, you're going to give me what I want."

Then he moved back, giving Bishop room to work. The mage set up a circle around Shiloh, the black salt closing around her bound form was bisected with sigils drawn in blood, the scarlet runes common enough that I knew exactly what they meant. And those connotations chilled me to the bone.

"I knew there was something wrong with you," Shiloh spat as she watched him carefully draw each symbol. "From the moment I met you, I knew you were just as sick, just as fucked-up as your boss. Now look at you, simping for another master. What, you can't stand on your own two feet? You too scared?"

Bishop stood mid-sigil, pointing his bloody fingers in her face. "You're lucky we need you alive for this, witch. But don't worry. I'm sure Nero won't have a problem with me taking the leftovers after he's done with you."

Shiloh tossed her head back and laughed like Bishop hadn't just threatened her with the worst sort of torture. "Tell me—did you lick his boots before or *after* he put them on your neck?"

But Bishop let her have that parting shot and went back to his sigils.

Sloane? Little sister? I know you can hear me. I know you said you only stay out of things because you're looking out for me—if the outcome will be worse if you don't. I get it. But please don't let them torture her. Please don't make me watch her die. Please come.

The little glimmer of hope I had in my chest died each second no one came. And that's when I knew no one would be coming to save us. No one was going to find us. No one was going to stop this.

Gritting my teeth, I tried yanking at my bonds, the metal shackle at my wrist biting into the flesh so tightly, I could barely move it. Plus, with every millimeter I shifted, the burning agony of Nero's torture nearly made me pass out.

No passing out. Shiloh needs you. Even if it is to just be a witness.

Shiloh met my gaze across the stage, the fear in her eyes clear, even this far away. I thought about all the times we'd worked together before I knew she was family. As someone who didn't have much of that left, I wished we would have spent more time getting to know each other. More time as friends rather than just as work acquaintances.

More time as family not in the middle of death or destruction.

And now we weren't going to have any of it.

As much as I wanted to see my father again, as much as I wanted to hug him one more time, as much as I needed to know he was okay, I wanted to live more.

I wanted breath in my lungs and fire in my blood. I wanted more from this life than just the shitty hand I'd been dealt.

All too soon, Bishop finished his preparations, moving back to Shiloh with a wicked blade in his hand. Just as he'd done in the caves, that blade was made of his dark death magics, formed from nothing but his power. He fit it under her chin, tilting her head up so she would meet his gaze.

"Any last words?"

Her smile was bitter yet determined. "I won't give my power to him. And you can't make me. You can't use your little blood magic to sway my mind, and you have no leverage over me."

Nero strode closer. "Oh, I think we do. Did you think we just stopped keeping tabs on you when you left Knoxville?" He tilted his head to the side, exposing the ruined skin on his neck. He was deteriorating and quickly. "This plan is centuries in the making, sweetheart. I've been keeping track of you since you burnt down half of Knoxville in the 1800s. You think that little *binding* kept you hidden from me?"

He walked his fingers up her sternum, *booping* her nose like a particularly precocious puppy. "What was your body count that time? Three hundred? A thousand? I forget." Nero shook his head, tutting at the witch. "And you think you're so much better than me."

"I was a child," she spat. "I had no control."

"Speaking of control," Nero said, his smile a touch wrong, "tell me how your cousin Jasper is doing these days. I hear she's got a nice new beau. And what about Poppy? Keeping her hands out of trouble? I wonder if she would like other kids to play with. I do so love my children."

Shiloh had been staying with her cousin Jasper in Georgia over the last month, hiding out after her "death." And Poppy was an orphan that Shiloh had taken under her wing once the coven collapsed—a St. James witch without a place to call home. As a psychometry witch, the ten-year-old was formidable, even before puberty. I'd found her with Bishop, saved her life, damn near dying in the process.

It would just figure that bastard would spill all our

secrets. That he'd tell the crazy asshole about the kid he'd found in the woods.

And Nero wanted her for his own.

Like a collectable.

Like a trophy.

Bile rose in my throat as I tried and failed to yank at my bonds, the thick leather belt across my middle holding me up and preventing me from wiggling too much. I was equally grateful and loathed that belt. Otherwise, I'd have to try and stand. Considering Nero had sliced me up like a two-day-old ham, standing was off the menu.

So was walking. Or fighting. Or getting out of here.

Hell, I was still bleeding, the slow trickle of rapidly cooling blood, oozing from my still-open wounds. But he wouldn't touch so much as a hair on Poppy's head. Over my dead body would he hurt her. Unfortunately, I figured that was the case no matter how the outcome played out.

"Leave them alone," Shiloh hissed, her eyes shining with tears as reality set in.

Nero seemed to delight in her misery. "I could. For a price. Give your power over to me, unleash the chaos bubbling under your skin, and in turn, I will leave Jasper and Poppy be. Don't? Well, it's only a six-hour drive to Whispering Waters, if I recall."

He wasn't bluffing or exaggerating. He would hop in a car and drive all the way to Georgia just to fuck with her family and not even bat an eye. He'd probably take all his creepy children with him, too.

He'd need a fucking bus for that, though. My gaze drifted to our audience, the red-robed children that were anything but. As messed up as I was, as much as I hurt, I could still feel their souls. Each one vibrated with the flavor of centuries, each one so much like Ingrid, it made me sick.

She wasn't the only one he'd turned. No, it looked like he had a collection of them, all blonde-haired, all blue-eyed, all fine-boned. She might have been the first, but she wasn't the last.

"I'll do it," Shiloh hissed through gritted teeth. "Leave them alone, and I'll give away my power."

"No," I shouted, struggling more against my bonds. "You can't give it to him. You *can't*."

If I endured hours of torture to keep Aemon from becoming a Nero puppet, the least she could do was stand up to these assholes.

She met my gaze, a smile half-forming on her lips. "Don't worry, Darby. It'll all work out." Blackness flooded her eyes, taking over the white. "You'll see."

At that, Bishop began to chant, his Latin flowing off his tongue with the practiced ease of a man that used the language every day. A year ago, he'd lied to my face when he'd told me he never used necromancy spells. That they were monitored and forbidden. As soon as he started spitting Latin like he was a Roman himself, I should have known something wasn't right.

"Repeat after me," Nero instructed her as Bishop and the children joined in on the chants. "I will my power to you to do with as you will. So mote it be."

Shiloh's eyes filled with tears as she looked right at me. "I-I will m-my power to y-you to do w-with as you will. So m-mote it be."

"Again."

She gritted her teeth, twin trails of tears falling down her cheeks. "I will my power to you to do with as you will. So mote it be."

"Again."

She thrashed, a cry of agony ripping up her throat before Bishop's blade fit under her chin again.

"Say it, witch."

"I will *all* my power to you to do with as you will," she growled, the vibration and timbre of her voice reaching me all the way across the room. "Make them pay. So mote it be."

Blackness bled from her eyes, traveling through those awful veins down her face and neck, forming a ball at the center of her chest. The sphere wrenched itself from her body, floating in a beautiful and strange orb that was both the darkest of blacks, and yet, held so much light it made my eyes hurt.

It bobbled there for a moment as a hush fell over the room, all breath, all thought paused for just a moment.

Then that darkness zoomed to me, hitting me right in the chest with the weight of a tidal wave. The pressure broke my bonds, the metal and wood flying as I soared backward. I'd thought I'd felt pain before. Thought Nero's torture was the worst I'd ever felt. Or maybe the souls of too many dead filling my flesh. Maybe Aemon's healing.

But no.

Shiloh's chaos burrowing into my skin, filling me with that darkness beat them all by a mile.

I screamed—so loud and so long that the sound didn't have meaning. But my scream was a single word —one I'd been so careful not to say. Not when Nero cut me to ribbons. Not when I wanted to die.

But in that darkest of moments, his was the only name I wanted to say.

Aemon.

20

Chaos was a funny thing. It was pure, unadulterated power. It could level a city or demolish a country. It could also build bridges, save lives, create a community. Humans and arcaners alike thrived in a small part in the midst of chaos. They needed it.

This was not that.

Shiloh's power filled my body, ripping through every cell, every muscle—racing through every organ and vein. It was rage and pain and vengeance. It invaded every thought, and with nowhere else to go, the magic wreaked havoc on everything around me.

The windows I had yet to notice shattered and blew in, raining glass on everything. The stone walls that I hadn't so much as looked at twice rumbled, each brick cracking as they rattled together. The ancient vampires in children's bodies scattered, their shrieks of alarm barely reaching my ears. The seats Nero's children had sat on toppled over, the metal screeching as it twisted. The floor itself broke apart, great fissures ripping through the rough wood, as if an earthquake was tearing the building in two.

My body dangled high in the air as the magic spilled out of me, touching everything and everyone. I wasn't meant to have this power. I—St. James blood or no— was not meant to hold this. But as much as it hurt, it healed, too. Bones righted, cuts closed, ligaments mended themselves. I ripped the metal bonds from my wrists, watching as my raw flesh healed before my eyes.

The room shook, the stage breaking apart like dry kindling as a strange light emanated from the rift in the floor. I lost sight of Shiloh, the cross she was tethered to falling from the platform and into the teeming crowd.

An odd scarlet and orange aura poured from the ground as flames flickered up and out of the crack. Horrible moans overtook the rumblings, the sounds straight out of the pits of Hell itself. A pair of hands emerged from the fissure, a familiar blond head rising from the pit as he answered my call.

Glowing red eyes found mine, his flaming horns

curling from his head as a shroud of smoke clung to his shoulders like a cape.

Aemon.

Beside him stood two equally tall and broad figures. One was dark-haired with a flaming crown weaved around his bone-like horns. He conjured blazing twin axes from thin air, as a roar of pure rage erupted from his mouth.

The other had long scarlet hair that fell down his bare back, stopping at the waist of his leathers. Shiny, obsidian horns curled in spirals from his crimson hair, matching his wicked talons. His bronze skin gleamed in an odd shimmering pattern, almost as if he had scales embedded into his flesh. His thick, tree-trunk legs stomped from the fissure, breaking the floor apart with each step.

A guttural language fell from Aemon's lips, and everyone froze for a split second. One moment vampires were crawling all over each other to flee, and the next, they all stopped as if they were playing the demon version of "Red light, Green light."

Then the redhead shifted, growing larger as his limbs changed shape. His head widened, his obsidian horns multiplying as his hair fell away and scales grew in its place. A few seconds later, a twenty-foot-tall dragon stood where a man had once been. It let out a roar that shook what was left of the walls, the stone crumbling as the vibrations tore them apart.

The dark one spat out an order in that same guttural language Aemon used, and then the room as a whole *moved*. Nero's children ran screaming, falling all over each other to escape, while Nero and Bishop and several older vampires moved in attack formations close to the edge of the broken platform. Nero's lieutenants rushed the demons, wielding red magic like their spells would do anything against residents of Hell itself.

But I wasn't going to let these murderers leave. I didn't care if the vampires hadn't done anything to me personally. Those little fuckers had planned on just sitting there and watching as their sire ripped Shiloh apart—ripped me apart.

No. Not on my watch.

They were going to burn right along with their master—along with their entire line, and when I was done, no one would remember the name Nero.

That rage that had ignited in my chest fell from my hands, pouring out of me as I sealed the room shut. I couldn't be sure exactly *how* I did it, but in my head was the knowledge that it had been done all the same. They climbed over each other like rats attempting to abandon ship, and with the utmost glee, my feet found the floor.

With a flick of my wrists, flames bloomed over the

edges of the room, engulfing tapestries, and tearing through curtains like dry kindling. The fire jumped from one to the next, heading for the stage as if guided by a hand. Picking my way through rubble and detritus, I followed the fire, not caring if it burned me. I had a sneaking suspicion it wouldn't. A small part of my brain predicted it would caress my skin like the softest of touches but burn anything and everything else.

The corner of my mouth lifted, a small flicker of joy sparking in my chest.

Nero and Bishop and all of these ancients would pay for their crimes. They would plead for death by the time I was done with them, and when she came, she would reap their souls from their bodies and deport their sorry putrid souls to Hell.

And if she couldn't carry them all, well, I was pretty sure she had backup.

Aemon and his friends spread out, taking on the hybrid vampires and their magic. Aemon dissolved into inky smoke, the flames of his eyes and horns the only thing I could track through the crowd.

But it was the crowd itself that was giving me trouble. Every soul called to me, especially the ones still trapped inside living vessels. Whispers of vengeance tickled my ears, begging me to yank those souls right out of their little bodies. More, I wanted to watch each and every one of them squirm as I pulled their very beings from them, witness their eyes go round and their mouths scream.

I was wrath personified.

Then another, smaller voice inside of me said a single name before it all came flooding back.

Shiloh.

She's hurt. Forget your vengeance. Remember her.

My humanity, my soul, my conscience. It was all there, bubbling up to the surface. A light in this darkness of chaos. Instead of heading for Bishop or Nero or even one of those magic-wielding lieutenants, I raced for the witch who'd gifted the very essence of herself to keep us all safe.

The problem lay with Nero's children. As soon as they found themselves locked in this place, they decided fighting was a far better option than just trying to escape. Small, blonde, childlike vampires descended on me en masse as I headed for Shiloh, their tiny mouths biting into my flesh like the parasites they were.

The pain should have registered, but it didn't. No, all I felt was rage.

Flames spilled from my hands, engulfing the little bastards like the ancient dried-out husks of the humans they once were. Specters began filling the room, their souls fleeing from me to avoid the fate their actions wrought. With Shiloh's magic added to mine, I didn't need to absorb them to know what was in store for their afterlife.

My path clear, I picked up speed, heading for the fallen witch who had to be hurting. I found her under a pile of splintered boards, her wrists broken, her head bleeding, her essence... *human.*

Then it all made sense. She hadn't just given me her chaos—she'd given me everything that made her a witch. All her magic, all her abilities.

Every ounce of the arcane.

"What did you go and do that for?" I whispered, brushing the bloody hair off her cheek.

With a snap of the flimsy metal, I shattered the cuffs at her wrists and ankles and pulled her from the rubble. Her spirit was so quiet now, the buzz of life that used to fill her muffled without the magic filling her veins. And that had me worried.

Quiet souls meant only one thing. Death was coming.

Not today, Shi. Not today.

With my own magic, I called for the souls that had just run from me, yanking them back bit by bit as they tried and failed to claw away. And when they finally fell into me, I ignored their lives and the horror of their misdeeds and gave what I could to Shiloh. Her wounds mended, her cuts sealing shut, but her eyes didn't flicker.

Yanking at the souls again, I took another one, passing the energy on as if I were a conduit. Then another. She startled in my arms, her eyelids fluttering as she sucked in breaths.

A shadow loomed over me, and I moved, protecting the vulnerable Shi behind me as a blade of pure magic formed in my hand, its golden light lengthening like a sword ready to strike. And strike I did. Without thought I slashed, and the edge clashed with the ax of Aemon's friend.

A hint of a smile hit his severe features before he uncrossed our blades and gestured to my now-human cousin? Friend? *Whatever.* His guttural language spilled from his lips, but even though I couldn't understand him, his brow was smooth, and his voice was kind.

I shook my head. "I don't understand you."

He tipped his chin up and then snaked around me, pulling Shiloh from the floor as he cradled her in his arms. "Help," he rumbled in broken English. "I help her. Keep safe."

He didn't wait for me to agree, he simply turned his back and disappeared into a cloud of smoke, taking Shiloh along with him.

My mouth dropped open in protest for a solid

moment, the confusion and roar of the battle warring in my brain for top dog. Did a demon from Hell just kidnap my friend?

But as soon as Shiloh's safety was moderately taken care of, the switch in my brain flipped, reminding me of a mage who'd earned my wrath and the vampire who needed killing.

I spotted Nero's sore-filled skin across the broken stage, fighting for his life against an enraged Bishop. The mage's dark magic streaked across his skin, staining his flesh with decay and rot.

Oh, good. A package deal.

Smiling, I waded into the battle. The blade in my hand fit my fingers perfectly, the magic humming with the desire to take life. The first time it cut through a vampire's neck, I started laughing, reaping his soul as soon as it left his body. I ignored the voice in the back of my mind that cautioned against taking too much or cringed at the horrors his spirit had.

Puking on my bare feet wasn't going to help anyone now, would it?

Tiptoeing through the debris, I let that blade fly, enjoying the slashes and parries, glutting myself on souls as I cut through the throng to get to my prize. The ground beneath my feet quaked, and the walls continued to crumble. The roar of an actual dragon

244 | ANNIE ANDERSON

echoed through the cavernous hall, and the fire blazed on.

Soon there was no one in between me and my prizes, but unfortunately, said prizes were in the midst of battle with one another.

I contemplated attempting to conjure popcorn just so I could watch them kill each other, but I figured with the whole battle going on and everything, it would be considered bad form.

Plus, I had a mage to kill.

Said mage was spitting Latin incantations left, right, and center, his purple and black magics trading back and forth with Nero's stolen ones. But Nero didn't know how to wield his pilfered power, the brute strength of it fizzling out as Bishop's words grew louder. His blackened hands latched onto Nero's shirt and a sickly gray light seemed to unfurl from the vampire's chest.

Oh, no, the fuck you don't.

Abandoning my watch and wait stance, I sprang forward, ripping the vampire right out of Bishop's hold, cutting off whatever spell he'd been using to steal the vamp's powers. Personally, I liked them right where they were: stuck in Nero's rapidly decaying body. The last thing I needed was a suped-up mage with an ax to grind, gaining more power. That seemed like poor planning and all that happy horse shit.

"Hiya, Bishop," I quipped jovially, my smile wide as realization dawned on his face that I'd foiled his plans. "Am I interrupting something?"

It was so funny to me that a few hours—hell, even a few minutes—earlier, I'd been terrified of what he might do to me. Now I was positively giddy at what I might do to him. It was an odd thing, the dominance of it all. Now that I was no longer at a disadvantage, I didn't care that he was in this room. I reveled in it. Because him being here meant I could kill him.

It meant every kiss and every touch would die with him. Every lie, every half-truth, every betrayal. They would all crumble to ash when he did.

And I. Couldn't. Wait.

"You stole that magic. It belongs to me," he spat, an orb of black death in his hand.

My lip pulled into a fake pout as I tilted my head to the side. "Oh, does it? Weird. Kind of looked like you were stealing it from someone else, but who can tell these days, right? So confusing."

Rather than argue with me, he lobbed that ball of rancid death right at me. A few days ago, I'd be ducking, but today? I caught it midair, letting the putrid, dark magic die in my palm as I closed my fist around it.

Holy. Fucking. Chaos.

No wonder Shiloh kept this shit under wraps. Every

Tom, Dick, and Harry in a thousand-mile radius would be trying to snake this power.

"Ooh, sorry," I taunted, unable to keep the smile off my face. "Having trouble keeping it up? Go ahead. Try again." It was a threat and a promise all rolled into one.

Bishop's golden eyes narrowed as he gritted his teeth, his banter nonexistent—the only thing left was the threats. "I'll see you dead, Adler. And when I do, I'll pick my teeth with your bones."

"Sure you will, sweetheart," I murmured, letting the power I already had coil in the air with the magic gifted to me. Golden light swirled with blackness, as I readied my blade. "Keep telling yourself that."

With a snide smile, another orb of magic formed in his hand, only this time, he didn't throw it at me. No, he pitched it straight into the ground, the blast knocking me off my feet. I flew backward, my back kissing rubble as I struggled to breathe.

As soon as blessed air filled my lungs, I was up and ready to fight. Only, when the dust cleared, I realized what he had done. The little bastard had fled. Used a distraction and just escaped.

I totally should have seen that coming.

Rage erupted from my throat as the earth quaked beneath my feet. Magic exploded from me, my fury ripping through the sea of Nero's progeny. The air filled with ashes as the vampires expired, and through the crowd, I saw a familiar face holding Nero still.

Aemon held the ancient vampire by the throat, a smile stretching his lips wide as he surveyed his prey. Nero was the reason Aemon had been locked in that box. Two thousand years of prison. The glee in Aemon's expression was a thing of beauty.

A commotion at the back of the room yanked my gaze away, and I had the immense pleasure of watching Ingrid—pigtails, sparkly shoes, pink jacket, and all— absolutely mowing through Nero's lieutenants like a one-woman wrecking ball. As per usual, she didn't carry a weapon, choosing to take her vengeance with her bare hands.

Behind her was Björn, his bald head on full display, and filigreed wand in hand, deflecting magic from his charge as she obliterated everything in front of her. Together they cut across the room, converging on Aemon and Nero. With joy, I watched as my friend surveyed her sire dispassionately, not letting him see the fear she'd had stored up for two thousand years.

Good girl, Ing. Man, I wish Mags could see this.

Honestly, I wished Thomas could, too—even as much as I despised the vamp. They had been with her the longest, had saved her from Norway before it was even a country. Got her away from Nero before his influence in Europe was too solid to surmount.

They would love to see her face this asshole.

Aemon twisted Nero in his grip, offering him to Ingrid like a sacrifice. As fucked as it was, it was probably the kindest thing he could have done. There were so many that needed their pound of flesh from that man, but both Aemon and Ingrid had been in prison for two thousand years, just of a different making.

Nero sneered at my tiny friend, his flesh decaying his lips making the expression lopsided. But Ingrid didn't say a word, didn't hesitate.

No, she reached up and snatched Nero's heart right out of his chest, crushing it to ash in her hand while he blinked once, twice, and then his body dissolved in Aemon's hold. But killing his vessel was only step one. Now it was time to reap his soul.

The dark specter that had once been a living Nero tried and failed to claw its way out of Aemon's grip, the prince's hold not faltering even a little. With a fair amount of relief on his face, Aemon dissolved into smoke, wrapping his body around Nero's putrid soul, and then disappearing altogether.

For some reason, disappointment filled my chest at seeing him go. Now that Nero was out of the picture, I probably wouldn't see the demon anymore. But at least someone got their happy ending. I was still stuck looking for mine. And by happy ending, I meant Bishop's head on a platter, but whatever.

Pouting, I took solace in watching a demon-dragon thing as it ate vampires, the last stragglers of Nero's line nothing more than dragon kibble. I sort of wanted to approach Ingrid, but I was still processing my disappointment.

Well, that and my absolute lack of purpose. There wasn't much left to kill, and I had all this power.

All dressed up and nowhere to go.

"You look rather put out," a familiar voice murmured in my ear, nearly making me jump out of my skin.

Turning, I spied Aemon, his expression unbothered, jovial even. "Well, my prey flew the coop. I guess my room-sealing skills aren't up to snuff."

Considering Ingrid and Björn got in the joint with no fuss, and Aemon's buddy got Shiloh out, and… Okay, a witch I was not. What did I know about sealing anything, but a chip bag closed?

Aemon tilted his head to the side, his smile widening. "I wouldn't worry too much about the magic. Summoning three Princes of Hell to the mortal world is nothing to sneeze at."

Eyes wide, my gaze fell on the dragon as it shrunk, reforming into the shape of a man.

250 | ANNIE ANDERSON

"That's your…" I trailed off, unsure how to classify the man who'd just flip-flopped from dragon to dude.

"Brother. Zephyr. He's a little rough around the edges. A little out of touch with humans, but he's good people. The one who took Shiloh is Bael. He's… *less* friendly, but still not too bad."

Considering they'd both stayed to fight even after I'd *summoned* them by accident, I'd say so. "Circle back to the summoning thing. If I recall, I only said *your* name."

His smile widened even further as he waved his hand, extinguishing the sea of flames I'd created. "That's chaos for you."

Swallowing thickly, I nodded. I supposed it was.

At that moment, the doors to the room opened and a very solid Jay and Jimmy strode through them with a struggling Astrid stuck in their ironclad grip. Her gaze found me, her eyes lighting in fury.

"What have you done to my theater?"

Her theater? *Her* theater? As calmly as I could—okay, so not calmly *at all*—I picked through ashes and debris to have words with the redheaded witch bitch.

At five feet away, she opened her mouth, but I didn't hear a word. And just like last time, when I landed my fist right in her jaw, I pulled my punch.

21

"You see, it wasn't my fault," Astrid insisted, her wide, pleading eyes doing nothing to stop the sheer level of rage that had me fighting against Aemon's hold.

The demon had both arms wrapped around me from behind. To anyone else, we might seem like an affectionate couple or that I needed support. To everyone else who knew better, I was a millisecond away from murdering a councilmember in front of said council.

I'd been too kind earlier. I should have just killed her instead of knocking her fucking lights out. The chaos teemed inside me, offering suggestions for just how we could fix this situation. On the docket were beheading, snapping her neck, disembowelment, ritual sacrifice... really, the options were limitless.

"Jaysus, Mary, and Joseph, that woman never shuts up, does she?" Hildy remarked, staring at the witch like he'd never seen someone so stupid. I kind of had to agree with him. Hildy had apologized profusely for not coming when I called, the anti-ghost spells Bishop had installed in Astrid's theater keeping him out. But he had told everyone where I was, so at least there was that.

"Nope," I muttered through gritted teeth.

Lise, Kato, Ingrid, and Reynard, plus the rest of the council—even her allies—stared at Astrid like she'd lost her mind. Lise pinched her brow, unable to fathom the stupidity any more than I could.

"You willingly gave information to a human who had been compelled to infiltrate the council. Then, you kept the murders to yourself for fear that someone might tip Nero off. You allowed your house and your coven to be overtaken." Lise let her hand drop and pinned the disgraced witch with her forbidding gaze. "You obstructed an investigation, sat idly by while a murderer walked free, and you have the nerve to claim it is not your fault?"

Okay, Hell had officially frozen over. Lise and I were on the same side for once.

Astrid shifted on her feet, the shackles at her wrists clinking with the movement. "Well, when you say it like that..."

Aemon's hold on me tightened, anticipating my movement as I tried to get free.

"Please tell me why I shouldn't let Warden Adler take your head right here, right now?"

I stilled, perking up at the thought of legally lopping her head off in the middle of this crowded room.

Astrid's mouth opened and closed like she was really trying to think of something that might save her ass. But she had no defense, not a single thing that could justify her actions.

"Personally, I think immediate execution is too kind," Reynard said, staring at the witch like she was worse than dog shit on his shoe.

Lise motioned for him to continue.

"She should be removed from the council and stripped of her magic, living the rest of her days as a human. She should forfeit all titles and assets. All monetary assets would be liquidated and given to the witches' families that lost their lives due to her incompetence." Lightning crackled over Reynard's hands as he sat forward in his chair. "*Then*, when she has nothing else but time, she should rot in prison for the rest of her miserable life." The lightning fizzled and cracked as he shrugged. "But that's just a suggestion."

"Now there's an idea," Hildy agreed. "Maybe some water torture thrown in for fun."

Kato bumped the druid with his shoulder as he swallowed an obnoxiously large bite of apple. "Oh, I approve. I do so love it when you're vicious, Rey. You should show your dark side more often."

Reynard rolled his eyes as he let a bit of his magic free, disintegrating the apple in Kato's hand right before he took a bite.

Kato's face fell. "Rude."

Lise's smile was small, but she seemed to enjoy Reynard's suggestion. "All in favor?"

Every single hand went up, and Kato, like the idiot he was, put up both hands.

"The ayes have it. Reynard, will you do the honors?"

Astrid tried to flee, but the shackles at her ankles made her trip. "No," she shrieked, trying to crawl away. "I did nothing wrong. You can't do this to me. I was tricked, can't you see that?"

Reynard stalked after the witch like a jungle cat, his eyes alight with wrath and his hand sparking with magic.

Granted, Preston *had* been a plant by Nero, so technically Astrid had been "tricked." But she was the one who ran her mouth off to a human in the first place. Had she kept her trap shut, several witches would still be alive.

The druid caught her by the ankle, reeling her in as

she screeched in protest. A moment later, the pair were out of the room, off to complete the ritual away from prying eyes. Personally, I didn't want to hear her scream and cry and pitch a fit, so the peace that settled over the room once her voice was gone was a blessing.

When the doors slammed shut, Lise's gaze fell on Shiloh and the demon prince behind her. The ancient blood mage's expression soured for a moment, but it cleared too fast for me to get a read on exactly what she was irritated about. "Ms. St. James, your sacrifice has been noted. If you would like to regain your power, I am positive Warden Adler would relinquish it to you. There is an open seat on the council for you as well."

Shiloh's lip curled as if she smelled hot garbage. "Me? A councilmember? Absolutely fucking not. In fact, I'm pretty sure I'd rather bathe in battery acid before I took that job. And the power you so freely think I want back can stay right where it is. Not a single bit of Knoxville or the covens or being a witch has brought me even one day of peace." She shook her head, taking a step back, her progress impeded by the demon at her back. "No thanks. I'd rather live a short human life than fall for that trap again."

That… was not what I was expecting she'd say. Sure, chaos was fun and all, but I was under the impression it would be a temporary thing instead of a permanent one. "Wait a minute here."

Shiloh shot me a pleading stare. "I gave it to you for a reason. I can't take it back. It isn't mine anymore."

Okay, first of all, I hadn't wanted the power in the first place. Second, it painted a teensy tiny target on my back. I already had enough trouble as it was. "But—"

Shiloh shook her head and then shot a look over her shoulder. Whatever Aemon's brother witnessed, it had to have been a signal because he grabbed the wi—err, *former* witch—and disappeared in a swirl of flames and smoke.

Perfect. Just perfect.

"Now that leaves you, Warden Adler," Lise began, and I could tell this was going downhill fast. "Please explain your summoning of not one, but three demons. Moreover, why have you not killed the demon you were assigned to deport?"

Was she high? She *had* to be to ask me that question.

I would have lost my shit, but the guarded council doors flew open, and Death and Torment decided to finally show up. Sloane and Deimos walked in side by side, with Bastian, Thomas, Sarina, Yazzie, Acker, and Tobin following behind them. I guessed the gang was all here.

My gaze narrowed on my sister, the rage and fear and

utter humiliation of Nero's torture bubbling up my throat. There was no way I could have kept my mouth shut even if I'd wanted to.

"Where the fuck have you been?"

Sloane's smile was knowing and repentant, meaning she wanted to come but couldn't for whatever reason Fate dictated. I was really getting tired of that bitch. Seriously. Fate could kiss my ass.

Did everything work out? Sort of. Nero was dead, sure. His followers were either ash or on the run. But Bishop was still out there, and I was stuck in the bullshit circle-jerk of a hearing trying not to go full monkey shit.

All things considered, the process left a fuck of a lot to be desired.

Ignoring me for the moment, Sloane let her dark wings free as she strode to the dais. "Lise Dubois, am I to understand that you are reprimanding my sister?"

Lise's face went white, and she dropped her gaze to the floor. "No. Simply asking a question."

"That's excellent. Because if you were, I'd have to start asking why you let a known heretic infiltrate your territory, poison your council, and murder your people. Not to mention that would bring up your grandson's involvement. But you're not, so I suppose I can keep my questions to myself, then?"

"That's right, lass. You tell her who's boss," Hildy

cheered, even though only Sloane, Aemon, and I could see or hear him.

Lise nodded, the emphatic movement so odd on the ancient mage's body. "If you wish, your eminence."

"Oh, I don't stand on ceremony, Madam Dubois. I do however have some suggestions, if you'd be open to them. It's none of my business, but I do have an in with Fate."

Christ on toast, Sloane was schooling this lady like she was born to do it.

Lise straightened in her chair, her gaze finding Sloane's. "Of course."

"You should not worry about any Prince of Hell on this plane. In a meeting with Deimos and the princes, we have all agreed that possession by higher demons is barbaric. All three of Deimos' sons have consented to be permanently bound to their current bodies. In turn, they are free to come and go on the mortal plane as they see fit. I suggest you learn to resolve any prejudices you have for that particular bloodline."

Gulping, Lise nodded. "Anything else?"

Slone's smile was pure feral. "Why, yes. I also suggest you abandon abolishing the ABI, and instead, instill qualified leadership. Sarina Kenzari is a perfect candidate for running the Knoxville branch, and under her command, I have a feeling they'll round up all of Nero's progeny in no time. Don't you agree?"

Lise shifted her gaze to the other council members, her eyebrows raised as if she was really thinking about it. Honestly, if Sarina was in charge of the ABI, being the Warden would feel more like a partnership instead of a prison sentence.

Ingrid rolled her eyes, sitting back in her chair as her feet dangled inches from the floor. "Oh, please. Sarina would clean house and get the Knoxville ABI out of the gutter after Mariana trashed it. I approve, and anyone with half a brain cell does to."

Lise's gaze shifted to the oracle, approval stamped all over her. "What do you say, Director? Want to 'clean house'?"

Sarina stepped around Sloane's wings, approaching the council. "Absolutely."

The blood mage nodded. "I'll let the intermediate director know of his replacement. Anything else?"

It made me furious that no one seemed to give a shit that Bishop was on the loose. It was "ABI this" and "Nero that" and "What about Astrid?"

What about the man who made the destruction and murder possible? What about the man who stole powers from innocent witches and helped drain ley lines? What about that guy?

"Oh, I've got something," I growled, elbowing Aemon in the gut when he didn't let me go. Free to move, I stalked toward Lise. "Bishop La Roux is free. After all he's done." The plan came to me on the spot. "I'm leaving Agents Yazzie, Acker, and Tobin in charge, along with help from Cooper and Hanson. They will run the Warden affairs while I hunt your grandson down. And once I'm done and I've cut off his fucking head and handed you his ashes, then I'm going on vacation."

Lise's face went white again, and she opened her mouth to protest.

I held up a hand. "This is *not* a debate. I'm not asking. I'm telling."

A week ago, the death mage to Lise's left insisted that I was a demigod and could do whatever the fuck I wanted. Well, I was taking his advice.

Spinning on a heel, I blew Jay and Jimmy a kiss, gave a finger wave to Deimos, and marched out of the council room with my head held high.

I was going to tie up this one loose thread, and then, I was taking a break. And heaven help anyone who got in my way.

A presence to my left had my steps faltering for a second until I recognized the signature of his soul. Rolling my eyes, I shot him a glare and stomped to a stop.

Aemon's smile was boyish and innocent. I didn't believe it for a second. As if he anticipated my wariness, he waggled his eyebrows as he stuffed his hands into the pockets of his suit pants.

"Want some company?"

"Sure." I shrugged, letting the chaos take the wheel. "Why not?"

Because there was no way teaming up with a demon could possibly go wrong.

Darby's story will continue with
Dead & Buried
Grave Talker Book Seven

———

Want to binge the sister series?
Don't miss **Night Watch**!
Available on Amazon & Kindle Unlimited!

DEAD & BURIED

Grave Talker Book Seven

Get ready for Darby's next adventure that will have you clinging to the edge of your seat.

Full blurb coming soon!

Preorder Now!

Coming February 21, 2023

Want to get to know Darby's sister? Check out...

NIGHT WATCH
Soul Reader Book One

Waking up at the foot of your own grave is no picnic... especially when you can't remember how you got there.

There are only two things Sloane knows for certain: how to kill bad guys, and that something awful turned her into a monster. With a price on her head and nowhere to run, choosing between a job and a bed or certain death sort of seems like a no-brainer.

If only there wasn't that silly rule about not killing people...

Grab Night Watch today!

SPELLS AND SLIP-UPS

The Wrong Witch Book One

I suck at witchcraft.

Coming from a long line of famous witches, I should be
at the top of the heap. Problem is, if there is a spell cast
anywhere in my vicinity, I will somehow mess it up.

As a probationary agent with the Arcane Bureau of
Investigation, I have two choices: I can limp along and
maybe pass myself off as a competent agent, or I can
fail. *Miserably.*

Worse news? If I can't get my act together, I may not only be out of a job, I could also lose my life.

Whose idea was this again?

Preorder now!
Coming July 5, 2022

THE ROGUE ETHEREAL SERIES

an adult urban fantasy series by Annie Anderson

Enjoy the Grave Talker Series?
Then you'll love Max!

Come meet Max. She's brash. She's inked. She has a bad habit of dying... *a lot.* She's also a Rogue with a demon on her tail and not much backup.
This witch has a serious bone to pick.

Check out the Rogue Ethereal Series today!

THE PHOENIX RISING SERIES

an adult paranormal romance series by Annie Anderson

Heaven, Hell, and everything in between. Fall into the realm of Phoenixes and Wraiths who guard the gates of the beyond. That is, if they can survive that long…

Living forever isn't all it's cracked up to be.

Check out the Phoenix Rising Series today!

JOIN
THE LEGION

EXCLUSIVE SNEAK PEEKS,
GIVEAWAYS, BOOK DISCUSSION.
COME FOR THE BOOKS.
STAY FOR THE MEMES.

To stay up to date on all things Annie Anderson, get exclusive access to ARCs and giveaways, and be a member of a fun, positive, drama-free space, join The Legion!

ABOUT THE AUTHOR

Annie Anderson is the author of the international bestselling Rogue Ethereal series. A United States Air Force veteran, Annie pens fast-paced Urban Fantasy novels filled with strong, snarky heroines and a boatload of magic. When she takes a break from writing, she can be found binge-watching The Magicians, flirting with her husband, wrangling children, or bribing her cantankerous dogs to go on a walk.

To find out more about Annie and her books, visit
www.annieande.com

Printed in Great Britain
by Amazon

40397740R00158